ZANE

INTERGALACTIC DATING AGENCY

DRAGON BRIDES
BOOK 13

KATE RUDOLPH

1

TWO SONS DOWN, one to go.

That was how Zane's parents had to see it. And his brothers. And his uncle, the king.

Him? No, he didn't see it that way at all. Rook and Vex could descend into happy matrimony as much was they wanted, but he would enjoy bachelorhood for at least another decade—or three.

What was the point of being the youngest if you didn't get to have some fun?

That fun was currently being curtailed by a certain determined matchmaker and a family summons that was impossible to ignore.

You will meet with Shade and hear her out. You will meet with the lady she chooses.

No "or else." There was no need when the person giving the ultimatum was the king.

It was days like these that Zane wished he was a normal dragon and not a lord. Normal dragons didn't need to meet with the allegedly psychic Royal Matchmaker and hear her out about potential brides.

Normal dragons got to … farm? Possibly? Own shops?

It occurred to him that he had no idea what normal dragons did all day. He should probably know that. As a lord, he was theoretically responsible for thousands of them. But that's what stewards were for.

Normal dragons probably didn't slum around Aetis, playing the tables, flirting with beautiful women, and winning and losing a fortune every night.

What miserable lives they must lead.

But Zane had a plan. He was good at plans. The youngest of three, he'd had to get good at plans as a child if he ever wanted to get one over on his brothers. Rook had brute force and Vex had strategy. Zane had learned to be creative.

It was pretty simple. He couldn't ignore the

king's summons. And at this early stage, he doubted he'd be forced into marriage. But there were only so many eligible ladies he could turn down before it became an issue.

So he'd just make sure she turned him down first.

Brilliant and simple, like all the best plans. And it started here in the outer shipyards on Aetis.

He'd been tempted to go to the lower city to find something truly seedy, but Zane wanted to actually survive the flight. The ships in the outer shipyards were in decent enough repair, and their captains could afford the security fees that kept the rabble at bay, but the captains there were also just a little desperate.

Perfect. Zane was just a little desperate too.

He passed by half a dozen ships trying to find something that would work. One was too new, another too shiny. He was pretty sure he owed money to the captain of another one, so that certainly wouldn't work. He made a mental note to send credits to the captain and hope that settled things between them. Zane paid his debts, but sometimes he could be a bit … forgetful.

There.

Perfect.

The ship looked flight worthy, if a bit dilapidated. The name ALTO appeared on one side, along with an identification number. There were dents and scratches, but it all looked cosmetic to Zane. A faded decal of what might have been a cheerful sun or possibly a fried egg was peeling off near the cargo bay door.

Exactly the kind of ship he'd never board.

The maintenance panels were mismatched colors, clearly scavenged from other vessels, and scorch marks decorated the underbelly. Someone had tried to clean them off but had given up halfway through. The landing gear on the port side had been welded at an angle that would make any proper mechanic weep.

It was the last place you'd find a wealthy, respectable Dragon Lord. He'd taken a first-class private transport to Aetis, where they'd served him meals on gold plates. Real gold, not plated. Utterly wasteful, and he'd loved every minute of it. It was possible this ship only had ration bars.

Was he really doing this?

Before Zane could decide otherwise, a human woman came down the gangplank and looked him over. Her eyes flicked up and down, expression completely unimpressed. She was short, with brown hair pulled back in a no-nonsense tie, serviceable gray pants, and black top, all covered by a bulky flight jacket.

The jacket had seen better days, patches at the elbows and a tear along one pocket that had been expertly mended. One patch was bright purple, clashing spectacularly with the jacket's faded olive green. Either she didn't care about aesthetics, or she'd grabbed whatever material was handy. Her hands were bare, showing calluses that came from manual work, not leisure.

She had the build of someone who shoved a ration bar into her mouth when her stomach finally screamed at her and slept even less. Sharp cheekbones, shadows under her eyes. But those eyes were alert, taking him in with the kind of assessment usually reserved for faulty engine parts.

Despite the utilitarian clothing, there was something about the way she held herself, the sharp intelligence in her green eyes, that made his focus narrow.

She moved with the economy of someone who knew exactly what her body could do and wasted no motion doing it. The scent of engine oil and metal clung to her, mixed with something else. Cheap soap. The industrial kind from station dispensers. And underneath that, the bitter tang of too much coffee.

His dragon, the part of him that usually only stirred for treasure or a good fight, perked up with interest.

Inconvenient.

"If you're slumming, go do it somewhere else." Her voice had the rough quality of someone who'd been breathing recycled air too long, each word clipped like she was rationing them. "This isn't a tour."

Zane grinned. "I'm not slumming, I'm looking to hire."

She raised her eyebrows and pursed her lips. The expression should have been dismissive, but there was calculation in it. She was already figuring out exactly how much she could charge him. Her gaze lingered on his boots. They cost more than her ship's fuel for a month.

Zane let himself slouch a little more. He'd dressed down for this, relatively speaking, but apparently not enough. "I have a meeting on Ofros, and I need a ride. You looked like you could use the fare."

The captain scoffed. "Do I look like a pleasure transport? Head to the upper decks for something a bit more your speed."

"I think you're exactly my speed."

She rolled her eyes. The motion was so thoroughly apathetic that it actually stung his pride a little. Women didn't usually dismiss him quite so easily. They certainly didn't look at him like he was a particularly annoying fly that had landed on their lunch.

Then she named a price.

It wasn't far off from what he'd paid for the ship with the gold plates. "Half up front in hard credit," she added. "You're not running from debts, are you?"

"No!" He definitely didn't glance back at the ship three berths down. That was merely a misunderstanding. "But you're insane if you think I'm paying that."

She shrugged. A single, economical movement that conveyed complete indifference to his financial concerns. "Then move along." She hopped off the gangplank and started towards the back of her ship. Her gait had the slightest hitch, favoring her left leg.

"Wait!" Zane didn't have time to argue, but now that he'd spotted this ship, he wanted it. No use finding something else. This was perfect. Exactly the kind of disaster his family would hate.

She stopped. Half-turned, one hand resting on her hip near what looked suspiciously like a concealed weapon. Her fingers drummed once against the grip. He wasn't sure if that was a warning or a habit.

"What's your name?" he asked.

She blinked a few times then answered, "Mercy Webb. Why?"

The name suited her. Short, practical, with just a hint of something more underneath.

"We appear to have gotten off on the wrong foot. I'm Lord Zane of Vemion, and I require transport to Ofros. Would you do me the honor of escorting me?" Already, his mind was turning with opportunity. Showing up in a busted-up ship with a beautiful human woman was exactly what he needed to do.

Shade would take one look at this situation and declare him unsuitable for any respectable match. Perfect.

She actually laughed. Not a polite titter or a charming giggle, but a genuine bark of amusement that transformed her face for just a moment. For a half-second, she looked younger. Less worn down by whatever had put those shadows under her eyes. "You definitely belong on the upper decks, Lord Zane."

"I don't need luxury," he insisted. "The only thing I require is fresh clothes and a suitable wine cellar."

Her expression went completely flat. "You're joking."

"About the wine? Never." He let his most charming smile spread across his face, the one that usually got him whatever he wanted. The one that had convinced a duchess to loan him her prize racing steed and a casino owner to extend his credit limit.

She was unmoved. If anything, she looked more skeptical. Her eyes narrowed slightly, like she was trying to figure out what con he was running.

She named her price again. This time with the air of someone who expected him to walk away. Her chin lifted just slightly. Daring him to balk. Good. Let her think she'd won this negotiation.

Was Zane really going to do this?

He thought of Shade's knowing smile. His mother's hopeful expression. The parade of suitable, boring, perfectly appropriate dragon ladies waiting to be paraded in front of him.

He thought of Mercy's unimpressed scowl and her rattletrap ship with its mismatched panels and questionable fried egg decal.

He smiled. "Where shall I send the credits?"

2

MERCY HAD MADE some stupid decisions about cargo before. The less she thought about that time she decided to transport an entire herd of cattle, the better. The smell had lingered for months, and she'd found hoofprints in places hoofprints had no business being.

Lord Zane, though, might have been the least wise decision she ever made, period.

He hadn't been kidding about the wine cellar.

Exactly forty-seven minutes after he climbed aboard with four large trunks and one small bag slung over his shoulder, he had summoned her to his room and politely requested her finest vintage.

Who did that? Lords, apparently. Lords who

wore silk shirts to travel through space and somehow made her cramped corridors feel smaller just by existing in them.

All Mercy had was half a bottle of something red she had picked up in a port she couldn't even pronounce the name of. The label had peeled off two years ago.

To Lord Zane's credit, he had drunk it down like the brave little lord he was. No grimace, no complaint. Just a slight tightening around his eyes that said he'd rather drink engine coolant. He hadn't asked for another glass with supper. He'd also left the bottle on the counter with exactly two sips of wine still in it, because apparently that's what lords did instead of just finishing the damn thing.

She wasn't sure how lords were supposed to act. Spoiled, sure. Vain, of course. Demanding, that went with the territory.

But when she walked through the galley after dinner on the second night and it was sparkling clean—far cleaner than she normally left it—she'd been confused. The metal surfaces actually gleamed. The recycler hummed contentedly instead of making that grinding noise that sounded like someone strangling a cat. Even the stubborn grease stain she'd given up on three months ago had vanished.

Had he smuggled a cleaning bot in with all of those supplies?

The third morning brought another surprise. Fresh bread. The smell filled the entire corridor, warm and yeasty and completely wrong for a cargo ship. She'd found him in the galley, flour dusting his expensive shirt, looking entirely too pleased with himself. He had a smudge of it on his cheekbone too, and she'd had to physically turn around to stop herself from pointing it out.

During lunch, she discovered more of his … helpfulness. "Where is the green spice?" she'd growled.

"It's in the cabinet right above the cooktop," Zane said, appearing at her elbow like some kind of silk-wearing ghost.

She nearly jumped out of her skin, spinning around, eyes wide and ready to lash out with the knife she had vowed to stop carrying two years ago. Her hand went to her hip where the blade used to rest, fingers closing on empty air. The movement was pure muscle memory. Old instincts died hard.

"You moved everything," she said.

"It makes more sense now."

Maybe to him. The old system had worked fine. Spices on the left, dried goods on the right, emergency rations hidden behind the false panel he thankfully hadn't found yet. She'd organized it during a three-day stint of insomnia, and the logic made perfect sense if you didn't think about it too hard.

"Things are where they are for a reason," she said. "You can't just go around moving things."

"And yet I did. Wine?"

He pulled out a bottle that she definitely hadn't seen before. The label was in a script she couldn't read, all elegant curves and gold leaf. It probably cost more than her fuel for this entire trip. The bottle itself looked hand-blown, with tiny imperfections that screamed "artisanal" and "your credit account is crying."

"Did you bring that with you?"

He shrugged. "I loaded up before climbing aboard. It was clear you weren't going to be honoring my demands about the wine cellar."

It wasn't a complaint. His mouth did this thing at the corner, not quite a smile, more like he was trying not to laugh at his own joke. Did he think it was funny?

What was this guy's deal?

She studied him. Three days in, and he still looked like he'd stepped out of some society holo. His hair fell in perfect waves, his clothes remained mysteriously unwrinkled. But there were shadows under his eyes she hadn't noticed before. Tension in the set of his shoulders when he thought she wasn't looking. And he had this habit of touching his left cufflink whenever he was about to lie or deflect. She'd clocked it on day two.

"So why did you need a ride?" she asked, taking the offered wine. It was offensively good. Smooth and complex, with layers of flavor that made her usual rotgut taste like battery acid. There was something in it that tasted like cherries, but also smoke, but also something else she couldn't name. It annoyed her that she liked it.

Zane shrugged and swirled his own vintage around in the tin mug he had scavenged from somewhere. "Life brings you to all sorts of places with all sorts of duties. I was summoned."

"Summoned for what?" She couldn't help but be curious.

He took a sip of his wine and didn't say more. His fingers found that cufflink again.

Okay, so that was off topic. But the way his jaw tightened at the word "summoned" told her someone had him by the metaphorical balls.

But he was a good drinking buddy. She found that out when he pulled out a deck of cards with edges so worn they felt soft as fabric and offered her more wine. He played with the casual confidence of someone who'd won and lost fortunes at the table.

His tells were subtle—a slight pause before a bluff, the way his thumb traced the edge of his cards when he had a good hand. She beat him anyway. Twice.

The next night, he set up the holo player, and they watched an old piece of media she'd been meaning to get around to. He'd laughed at all the right parts, made sarcastic comments that actually improved the terrible dialogue. For two hours, she'd almost forgotten he was a lord and she was just hired help. He'd also fallen asleep in the last fifteen minutes, his head tipped back against the wall, mouth slightly open. It should have looked ridiculous. Instead, she wanted to run her fingers down his cheek.

Not happening.

She had expected him to hole up in his room the entire journey and grit his teeth trying to get through this uncomfortable ride. Instead, it appeared he didn't like to be alone. He sought her out during meals, lingered in the cockpit asking questions about navigation, even helped with routine maintenance checks. His hands might be soft, but he wasn't afraid to get them dirty. Though he did have a weird thing about wiping them on a handkerchief instead of his pants like a normal person.

On the fourth day, everything went to shit. And surprisingly, it wasn't Zane's fault.

Mercy had just finished checking her daily readings when the proximity alarm went off. The sound cut through the quiet hum of the engines, sharp and insistent. The cockpit was bathed in a hellish flashing red. She checked every sensor she could, but none of them were showing anything wrong. Ghost signature. Either a malfunction or someone with very expensive cloaking tech. Her gut said expensive cloaking tech. Her gut was usually right about these things.

Zane rushed into the room. "What's that?" he asked.

"We're close to something, but I don't know

what. We're not near any sort of asteroid field or planet, and no ship should be close to us."

Her ship rocked, and the alarm got even more insistent. The Alto groaned, metal straining against forces it wasn't built to handle. She could feel the vibration through her boots. The kind of vibration that meant expensive repairs. If she lived long enough to make them.

"Strap in," she commanded him.

Mercy took over controls and tried to roll them out of whatever danger they were in, but no matter how hard she tugged on the joystick, her ship wouldn't move. The stick fought her, servos whining in protest. The familiar responsiveness of her ship was gone, replaced by dead weight. They were caught in some sort of tractor beam. And that meant only one thing.

"Pirates. Fuck."

Why would they target her?

She wasn't flying through dangerous lanes, and her ship wasn't exactly a prime target. The Alto looked like what it was—a working vessel barely worth the metal it was made from. She'd specifically kept it looking like shit for this exact reason. She looked over at her passenger.

Lord.

Yeah, that could be a problem. Everything about him screamed money, from his perfect teeth to the way he held himself. Even his fingernails looked expensive somehow.

"No one's after you, are they?" she asked.

"No," Zane insisted. "What kind of life do you think I live?"

The kind with silk shirts and hand-blown wine bottles, she thought but didn't say.

"We're already caught," she said. "Stay calm, and maybe they let us out of this. You might want to run and hide your valuables," she offered.

Of course, any pirate worth their career would take one look at him and realize just how valuable he could be. Ransom material. The kind that would set a crew up for years.

The ship rocked again, but Zane undid his security belt and bolted for his room.

Probably for the best. She needed to deal with this herself. Pirates responded to strength or submission, nothing in between. And she'd be damned if she was going with submission.

Her comm screen blinked with an incoming call. Close proximity. Her new friends.

Mercy accepted the call, and the screen lit up with a man she didn't recognize. He was human with dark hair peppered with gray, maybe about sixty or so. He had a mean scar on his face and a bulky build that told her he would be difficult in a fight despite his age. The scar ran from his left temple to his jaw. His eyes were cold and calculating.

"This doesn't have to be difficult," he said. His voice carried the confidence of someone who'd done this a hundred times before.

"There's nothing of value here," Mercy told him. She wasn't about to panic, but she was very aware that they could blow her ship to smithereens at any moment. Her ship. Her home. The only thing in the universe that was actually *hers*.

"I'll be the judge of that," said the pirate. "You can call me Horris. Now, do me the pleasure of giving me your name."

"It's Mercy," she said, though she wasn't begging for any yet.

Horris narrowed his eyes. "Full name, lady captain."

So he wanted formality. Whatever. "Mercy Webb, captain of the Alto. This is a simple transport ship, and there's nothing you could possibly want."

For some reason, that made Horris smile. "Now,

Captain Webb, you can open the doors for me and my men, or I can blast them off. It's your choice, but I will be boarding your ship. What's it going to be?"

Goddamn it. She was really hoping she could have talked them out of this, but maybe they needed to see that she was worthless for them-selves. Her finger hovered over the docking control. Once she pressed it, there was no going back.

She punched the button hard enough to make her knuckle hurt. "There," she said. "Dock away."

Horris gave her a vicious smile and cut off the call.

Mercy sat back in her seat and cursed. She let out one more god-fucking-shit-damn before pushing out of her seat. The familiar sounds of her ship were different now, violated. She could hear them attaching to her hull. Parasites.

Should she grab her blaster? It was tempting, but Horris had the upper hand, and he knew it. How many crew members did he have? She had Zane and had no idea if he could take a punch. He probably had never taken a punch in his life. Lords didn't get punched. They got "challenged to duels" or whatever.

She'd leave it hidden for now and hope she could get it later.

She got up and went to meet the pirate captain, every step feeling like she was walking toward her doom. The dock bay had never seemed so far away. She could hear the magnetic seals engaging, the hiss of pressure equalizing. The sound of her autonomy evaporating.

He was already on the ship when she got to the bay door, and Horris smiled when he saw her. Up close, she could see old burn marks and scars on his hands.

"This isn't exactly what I pictured when I met Rayden Webb's daughter," he said.

Her dad? The asshole who had abandoned her when she was a kid? What did he have to do with anything?

She hadn't heard that name in over a decade. The bastard had walked out when she was seven, chasing some grand adventure, leaving her and her mother with nothing but debts and broken promises. Her only gift from him had been a half-broken music box that played the same six notes over and over until she'd thrown it out at age fifteen.

Horris held up a hand and gestured forward, and four of his people boarded the ship. Two humans, a Kellian with scales that caught the light, and something she couldn't identify under the environmental suit. All armed. All moving with the coordinated precision of people who'd worked together for years.

"Take a look around," he told them. "We don't want any surprises. It's time for Captain Webb and I to have a little talk."

3

DRAGON FIRE WAS great until you were sitting in the middle of space about to face down pirate scum. Zane grimaced. One wrong move, one slightly too powerful gesture, and he'd cook the hull with all of them inside of it.

Some might be willing to take the risk, but not him. He actually wanted to live.

Was hiding an option?

The Alto wasn't built for it. Every corridor was narrow and utilitarian, designed to maximize cargo space, not provide sanctuary for wayward lords. The few storage compartments were obvious. His quarters held nothing but a bunk and his trunks. The engine room would cook him alive if he tried to squeeze behind the drive units. Even the maintenance crawlways were too exposed, with access panels that would take seconds to pop open.

No. He'd have to face this head-on. Somehow.

Damnation.

Boots thundered through the corridor outside his door. Multiple sets, moving with purpose. Not the casual stride of people exploring—these were hunters who knew exactly what they were looking for. Metal scraped against metal as they checked other compartments. A woman's voice, sharp and businesslike, called out clearances. They were being thorough.

"Two more doors on this level," someone said. Male and too close.

His dragon stirred beneath his skin, threatening to surface. The beast wanted to fight, to protect Mercy and … he didn't know where that thought was trying to lead. Zane forced it down. Not here. Not when his prickly captain could get caught in the crossfire. Not when she'd just started to smile at his terrible jokes.

He couldn't use his fire. He couldn't risk himself. He couldn't risk the ship. And he certainly couldn't risk Mercy.

He wasn't sure what he'd expected from the gruff transport captain, but it wasn't her sharp smile or the curious way her eyes would flick him up and down when she thought he wasn't looking. Or the way she'd beaten him at cards with this little smirk that made him want to lose again just to see it.

She smelled like engine oil and that clean soap she used, nothing fancy, but it had started to permeate his senses. It was in his quarters now. He'd noticed it this morning on his pillow and had spent a full minute trying to figure out how that had happened before remembering she'd helped him fix the air recycler yesterday. They'd known each other four days. But when she'd laughed at his terrible joke about the wine last night, genuine and unguarded, something in his chest had shifted.

With a pang, Zane let it go. There was no time to get caught up in could-have-beens with the pretty captain. He had to survive this first.

At least he had an excuse for why he was going to be late for his meeting with his matchmaker-selected lady.

Zane was huffing out a laugh as the door burst open and two pirates aimed blasters right for him. The barrels looked impossibly large from this angle, dark holes that promised nothing good. His first instinct was to fling fire their way, but he held back.

Until he knew where Mercy was, that she was safe, he couldn't do a damned thing.

"Don't shoot!" Zane threw his hands up and let his voice go high and reedy. He added a little tremor for effect. "I'm worth more alive than dead!"

The two pirates exchanged glances. The human one snorted. His face was weathered and scarred, the kind of man who'd spent years in the worst parts of space and come out meaner for it. "Look at this one. Soft as butter."

"Please, I have money. Lots of money." Zane let his hands shake. Just a little. Enough to sell it. He'd practiced this act before. Rich, useless lordling. It wasn't even that far from the truth.

The Kellian's scales rippled with what might have been amusement. "Captain Horris wants to meet you." The human gripped his upper arm tight enough to bruise and dragged him into the hall.

They marched him out at blaster-point. Zane made sure to stumble once, catching himself on the wall with a whimper. His muttered "oh dear" made the Kellian laugh and shove him harder. The pirates relaxed their grips on their weapons.

Good. Let them think he was harmless.

Mercy stood in the cargo bay with her chin up and her hands clenched at her sides. She looked pissed, but there was a tremor in her shoulders. A thin line of blood ran down her left arm from a fresh cut. The red was shockingly bright against her pale skin. The man who must have been Captain Horris loomed over her, close enough that Zane's dragon stirred with fury.

Too close. The bastard was standing in her space, using his bulk to intimidate. Mercy hadn't backed down an inch, but Zane could see the cost of that courage in the white-knuckled grip of her fists.

"Ah, the passenger." Horris turned. His movements were casual, confident, a predator who knew his prey was already caught. "Lord Zane, according to the manifest. How fortunate."

"I can pay you," Zane said quickly. "Whatever you want. My family has extensive holdings—"

"I'm not interested in your money, boy."

Boy? Zane bit back his real response. His jaw ached from the effort of keeping his expression meek. "Then what? I'm sure we can come to an arrangement."

Horris smiled. It wasn't pleasant. "Right now, I'm interested in Captain Webb here. You're ... an annoyance."

"I told you, I don't know anything about my father," Mercy said through gritted teeth.

Her father? Zane filed that away.

"Lock them up," Horris ordered. "The aft storage closet should hold them while we search the ship properly."

Two pirates grabbed Zane. He let them, making token protests but not resisting. "Please, surely we can discuss this like civilized beings—" They shoved him and Mercy into a closet barely big enough for one person, let alone two.

The door slammed shut, and the lock engaged with a decisive click.

The space was suffocating. Zane's back pressed against shelving units that dug into his spine, while Mercy was wedged against his chest, her head barely reaching his shoulder. He could count the individual threads in her shirt from this angle. He could see a small scar on her collarbone, maybe two centimeters long, silvered with age.

Every breath she took pressed her more firmly against him. The emergency lighting cast everything in a sickly yellow glow that made the shadows deeper and the walls feel even closer.

He could feel her heartbeat.

Fast but steady, drumming against his ribs. Her hair tickled his chin, and that clean soap scent was overwhelming in the confined space. Something floral. Cheap, probably, but it worked on her. She shifted, trying to find a position that didn't involve being plastered against him, but there was nowhere to go.

Her hip pressed into his thigh. Her hand landed on his chest for balance before she jerked it away like she'd been burned. Her palm left a warm spot on his shirt. He could feel the exact shape of it.

"Sorry," she muttered, the word ghosting across his collarbone.

"Are you hurt?" Zane asked quietly. He wanted to run his hands over her and feel for himself but resisted the urge. Barely.

"I'm fine."

She wasn't. In the dim emergency lighting, he could see the bruise darkening on her cheekbone. The cut on her arm was deeper than it had looked from across the cargo bay.

Every instinct screamed at him to tear through the door, to hunt down Horris and show him what happened to those who drew blood from his people. The fury was volcanic, threatening to consume his façade of uselessness. His skin felt too tight. His temperature was rising. He wanted to blow a hole in the door and murder *everyone*.

His hands trembled with the effort of not shifting, of not letting his claws extend and his scales surface.

But Mercy was watching him. Even in the bad light, her sharp eyes missed nothing. Those eyes that had catalogued every one of his tells in three days. But he couldn't risk her getting caught up in the violence of a fight. Pirates had backup plans. Dead man's switches. If he killed Horris, the rest of the crew might destroy the ship out of spite.

So he kept his voice weak, let his hands shake for different reasons. Played the pampered lord while everything inside him wanted to rage.

"I can offer them more money," he said, keeping his voice weak and uncertain. "My family—"

"Your money won't help." Mercy shifted, wincing. The movement brought fresh blood welling from the cut on her arm. "They want something to do with my father. The bastard's been gone for twenty years and he's still fucking up my life."

"What about your father?"

"Nothing. He left. That's all." Her voice was flat. Final.

Despite her steady voice, he could feel the fine

tremors running through her body where she pressed against him. Fear or adrenaline or both, carefully controlled but impossible to hide when they were this close. Her breathing had gone shallow.

"We need to get out of here," she said. "Can you fight?"

"I … I've had some training," Zane said carefully. "Self-defense lessons. Dancing. That sort of thing."

Mercy stared at him in the dim light. "Dancing."

"The waltz can be quite athletic."

"Get your shit together, Lord Zane. These are actual pirates. They will actually kill us."

"I'm aware of that."

"Then stop acting like a—" She cut herself off. Her eyes narrowed, studying him with an intensity that made his breath catch. "You can't actually be this useless."

His pulse jumped. She was too smart, too observant. His mind raced for a deflection, something to throw her off the scent. His hand found his cufflink. Damn it.

"I'm exactly as useful as I appear," he said.

She was quiet for a long moment. Her breath

whispered across his throat as she seemed to weigh his words. Her eyes dropped to his hand, still on the cufflink. Back to his face. "Right. Of course you are."

The sounds of destruction filtered through the door. Metal shrieked as panels were torn away. Glass shattered, probably the few personal items Mercy had in her quarters. That sound made her flinch. Something breakable, then. Something that mattered. Boots stomped overhead, and something heavy crashed to the deck. They were being thorough, systematic. This wasn't random looting.

"Check behind the nav console," Horris's voice carried through the walls. "These old ships sometimes have hidden compartments."

Mercy tensed against him. Her fingers curled into his shirt, an unconscious gesture that told him they'd find something she didn't want found. Emergency credits? Weapons? Whatever it was, the pirates were getting closer to it.

"How long before they realize you don't have whatever they're looking for?" Zane asked.

"Not long enough."

4

MERCY HAD BEEN PRESSED against plenty of people before. Crowded transport shuttles, packed marketplaces, the occasional bar crush right before it turned into a fight. But being wedged against Lord Zane in a closet the size of a coffin was something else entirely.

He was warm.

Too warm.

The kind of heat that seeped through clothing and made her hyperaware of every point of contact. His chest rose and fell against hers with each breath, steady despite their situation. She could feel the lean muscle beneath his ridiculous silk shirt, the strength he tried so hard to hide behind that pampered exterior.

And he smelled good. It was distracting as hell when she needed to be thinking about escape routes and weapon stashes.

"Your heartbeat's elevated," he murmured, and she could feel his breath stir her hair.

"We're about to die," she shot back. "Of course it is."

"Ah." The sound vibrated through his chest into hers. "That must be it."

Was he … was he flirting with her? Now? While pirates tore her ship apart looking for some mythical treasure map? The man had no sense of self-preservation.

She shifted, trying to find a position that involved less full-body contact, but only succeeded in pressing her hips more firmly against his. He made a small sound, quickly stifled, and she froze.

"Sorry," she muttered.

"No need to apologize." His voice had gone deeper, rougher. "Though if you keep moving like that—"

The door yanked open, flooding the tiny space with harsh light. Mercy blinked, momentarily blinded, as rough hands grabbed her arms and hauled her out. Her legs had gone numb from the awkward position, and she stumbled.

"Move it," one of the pirates growled, shoving a blaster against her ribs. Behind her, she heard Zane yelp before they slammed the door shut again.

They dragged her through her ship, and Mercy felt each bit of destruction like a cut of a knife. The panel she'd rewired last month hung open, its guts spilled across the deck. Her few personal items lay scattered and broken. The ceramic mug her mom had given her lay in three pieces near the galley entrance. Even the pilot's seat had been slashed open, foam stuffing bleeding out like innards.

She'd spent five years keeping the Alto running. Five years of scraped knuckles and late nights and careful budgeting to afford parts. This ship was her freedom, her home, her life. And they were destroying it for nothing.

"I really hate pirates," she said through gritted teeth.

The one holding her arm laughed. "Feeling's mutual, sweetheart."

They shoved her onto the bridge. Horris stood by her navigation console, running his fingers over the displays with casual control. Like he already owned everything there. Like she was just an inconvenience to be dealt with.

"Tie her to the chair," he said without look-ing up.

Mercy struggled, but there were too many of them. They forced her into the pilot's seat—her own damned seat—and wrapped cargo straps around her wrists. The straps bit into her skin, too tight for comfort but not quite tight enough to cut off circulation. They knew what they were doing.

Horris finally turned to face her. Up close, that scar was even uglier, pulling his mouth into a permanent sneer. "Now then. Let's have a civilized conversation."

"Hard to be civilized when I'm tied up." The words came out rough, her throat dry from fear and adrenaline. The cargo straps had already started to chafe, the synthetic material designed to hold ship-ping containers, not human wrists.

He backhanded her. The blow snapped her head to the side, and she tasted copper. Her vision went white at the edges, then filled with dancing black spots. Pain exploded across her cheek, radi-ating up into her temple and down her jaw. The metallic taste flooded her mouth, and she had to blink several times to clear the spots dancing in front of her eyes. Her ears rang with a high whine that made everything else sound muffled and distant.

"Where's your father?" he asked. He straightened his jacket, smoothing down the fabric like violence was just another part of his daily routine. His scarred face showed no emotion, no satisfaction or anger. Just cold calculation.

Mercy worked her jaw, then spat blood onto the deck. It landed with a wet splat near his boots.

"I haven't seen him since I was a kid. I have no idea. Dead, probably." She tested her teeth with her tongue, relieved to find them all still in place. The taste of blood was overwhelming, coating her mouth with copper and salt. Her cheek was already swelling.

"Don't lie to me."

"I'm not."

The truth rang in her voice, clear and sharp. She'd had twenty years to get over being abandoned. Twenty years to stop caring whether Rayden Webb was alive or dead or floating in some asteroid field. The anger had burned out long ago, leaving only hollow indifference.

Horris hit her again, harder this time. This time she saw it coming and tried to roll with it, but the straps held her in place.

The headrest cracked under the impact. Blood filled her mouth again, and she could feel her lip splitting. The taste made her stomach turn, but she swallowed it down rather than give him the satisfaction of seeing her spit again.

"This can be a discussion, or it can hurt." He leaned in close enough that she could smell the sour alcohol on his breath. "Your choice."

His face filled her vision, all scarred flesh and cold eyes. Her heart hammered against her ribs so hard she was sure he could hear it.

"Hitting me doesn't change the fact that I have no idea where my father is." She met his eyes, refusing to look away. "He walked out twenty years ago. If you want to find him, you're about two decades too late." Each word came out steady despite the way her voice wanted to shake. She'd learned a long time ago that showing fear only made predators circle closer.

Better to spit in their faces and hope they respected the fight, even if they killed you for it.

"Then where's the map?"

She blinked and looked towards the console. "The nav system's right there. You have all my maps."

His hand came up again, and Mercy couldn't

help but flinch. The movement seemed to satisfy him because he lowered it slowly. His mouth twisted into something that might have been a smile if it had contained any warmth whatsoever.

"What map?" She hated how her voice shook. "I have a standard nav package, it's not like I'm carrying paper star charts."

"The Map of Planetary Runes."

The name fell into the silence. Mercy felt her face go blank, expression shifting from pain and fear to complete bewilderment.

The words meant nothing. Absolutely nothing. Mercy stared at him, searching for some hint of what he wanted. "The what?"

Horris grabbed her shoulders and shook her hard enough to rattle her teeth. The straps cut deeper into her wrists. "Your father's treasure. He found the map. And now I'm certain he hid it with you. So give it to me and we can end this thing."

End this.

She knew exactly what that meant. A quick blast to the head if she was lucky. Something slow if she wasn't. Either way, she was dead the moment she gave him what he wanted.

Too bad she had no idea what he was talking about.

"My father walked out on me and my mom when I was seven." She kept her voice steady despite the tremor in her chest. "I have never heard of this map, and I have no idea what you're talking about."

His face darkened, and she braced for another blow. But before he could strike, one of his crew stumbled through the door, dragging Zane.

"What?" Horris snapped.

"He was wandering around, Captain." The pirate looked annoyed more than anything. Like Zane was a particularly irritating pest.

"I had to use the facilities." Zane's voice had gone high and whiny, with just a note of aristocratic outrage. He actually stamped his foot, the expensive boot making a hollow thud against the deck. "You can't expect me to just … hold it."

And that's when Mercy knew for certain he was faking.

Nobody was that stupid.

Nobody who'd helped repair her nav array two days ago, who'd spotted a potential coolant leak she'd missed, who played cards with the tactical awareness of a seasoned gambler.

This was an act, and he was selling it.

Hard.

His eyes found hers across the bridge. For just a moment, something dark and dangerous flickered in those brown depths. His gaze tracked over her face, taking in the swelling, the blood, the way she was tied. His jaw tightened almost imperceptibly. And for just a second, she could have sworn she saw smoke curling from his nostrils, thin wisps that dissipated before she could be sure they were real.

That must have been the concussion.

Then, just as quickly, the mask slipped back into place. He wrung his hands and shifted from foot to foot like a child.

"If you have to piss, piss in the corner." Horris waved dismissively. "Take him back, tie him up." He paused, seeming to remember she existed. "Take her too. We have work to do."

5

THE CLOSET HAD BECOME a special kind of torture after the first hour.

After what felt like a full day, Mercy's body screamed in protest with every breath. Her legs had gone from numb to burning to a deep ache that radiated up into her hips.

The shelving units dug grooves into her back that would probably leave permanent marks. Her wrists throbbed where the cargo straps had cut into them earlier, and her face felt swollen and hot. She couldn't touch it to assess the damage, but based on the way her left eye was starting to swell shut, she looked like hell.

But worse than any of that was the hunger. Her

stomach had given up growling hours ago, settling into a hollow ache that made her lightheaded.

When was the last time she'd eaten? Before the pirates. Before everything went to hell. The bread. Zane's bread, still warm from the oven, with butter melting into the crust. That felt like a lifetime ago.

She leaned against Zane because there was nowhere else to go. His arms had come around her at some point, holding her steady when her legs threatened to give out. The position should have been awkward, intimate in a way that crossed every professional boundary she had. But exhaustion had stripped away her ability to care about propriety.

His heartbeat was steady under her ear. Calm. How could he be calm?

"My fucking useless dad is going to get us killed." The words came out raw, scraped from a throat dry with thirst.

His voice rumbled through his chest, and she felt it as much as heard it. "We're not going to die."

Mercy lifted her head enough to look at him. His face was all sharp angles and shadows, nothing like the soft lord who'd complained about wine quality. Even in the dimness, she could see the certainty in his expression. Like death was simply not an option he was willing to consider.

"We're doing a great job of surviving right now." The sarcasm cost her. Her split lip cracked open again, and she tasted fresh blood.

"We've seen four pirates and the captain. There's almost certainly at least one more on their ship." He shifted slightly, adjusting his grip on her when she swayed. "We can take them."

Was he serious? She searched his face for signs of delusion brought on by oxygen deprivation, but his eyes were clear. Focused. Nothing like the bumbling lord who'd whined about bathroom breaks.

"I have a blaster hidden on the bridge." She'd stashed it behind a false panel near the pilot's seat three years ago after a close call with raiders. "But they'll kill me before I make it three steps." The image flashed through her mind. Her hand reaching for the weapon. The pirates faster, always faster. Blaster fire tearing through her before she could touch the grip. "Fuck!" The word exploded out of her. "I should have fought them when they showed up. I'm sorry, this is so bad."

This was her fault. Her ship. Her responsibility. She'd let them board, thinking she could talk her way out of it. Thinking they'd see she had nothing and leave. Stupid. So stupid.

"We don't need your blaster." His hand came up to cup the back of her head, gentle despite their situation. His palm was warm, almost hot, against her skull. "I can handle them, but I need you to be safe."

The touch should have been comforting. Instead, it sent a spike of anger through her exhaustion. Safe? She'd been taking care of herself since she was sixteen. She didn't need protecting.

"I can handle myself." She tried to pull back, but there was nowhere to go. "And you're my passenger. I'm responsible for your safety."

Not the other way around. She was the captain. He was cargo, valuable cargo who'd paid half up front, but cargo nonetheless. It was her job to get him to his destination intact.

"I can handle myself, too."

Something in his tone made her look at him again. Really look. Past the expensive clothes and once-perfect, now mussed and a little greasy hair. Past the act he'd been selling since the pirates grabbed them. There was something there, lurking beneath the surface.

Something dangerous.

They lapsed into silence. Her mind turned over his words, trying to make sense of them. What kind of lord could "handle" armed pirates? What was she missing?

Time crawled by. Minutes or hours, she couldn't tell anymore. The emergency lighting never changed, the walls never moved, and their bodies remained pressed together in forced intimacy. Her thoughts grew sluggish, focusing down to basic needs. Water. Food. Freedom.

The way Zane's thumb was tracing small circles on her shoulder, probably unconsciously. The heat of him seeping into her bones.

Then she heard it.

Running feet in the corridor outside. Shouts, muffled by the door but urgent. Angry.

The proximity alarm shrieked to life, cutting through the ship like a blade. The sound was different from inside the closet, muted but still sharp enough to make her flinch.

"What the hell?" She pressed her ear against the door, trying to make out words through the metal.

The pirates who'd attacked her sounded like they were about to be attacked themselves. The irony wasn't lost on her. Part of her, the petty part that was tired and hurt and angry, found it hilarious. Served them right.

Chaos erupted outside. More running. Something heavy crashed into a bulkhead. It cut off abruptly.

Zane moved. In the confined space, it took effort, but he managed to turn himself around so he faced the door. His body formed a barrier between her and whatever was happening outside. The gesture was so unconsciously protective that something twisted in her chest.

"What are you doing?" she whispered.

He didn't answer. His shoulders had gone rigid, every muscle tense. Ready. And the closet was getting hot. Or maybe she was imagining it.

Then she smelled it. Burning. Acrid smoke that made her nose wrinkle. But how? They were in space. Fire needed oxygen, and shipboard fire suppression systems were brutal in their efficiency. Any flame should have been smothered in seconds.

Had they been boarded? Was someone using incendiaries? Her mind raced through possibilities, each worse than the last.

The door yanked open, and she squinted against the sudden brightness. The corridor beyond was empty. No pirates. No boarders. Just wisps of smoke curling along the ceiling and a dark scorch mark on the wall that definitely hadn't been there before.

She and Zane stumbled out, her legs barely holding her weight. Pins and needles shot up from her feet with each step. She had to grab the wall to keep from falling, her hand landing in something wet and warm that she really didn't want to examine too closely.

"I think we have our moment." Zane steadied her with a hand on her elbow, already moving toward the bridge.

"What did you do?" The question came out sharper than she intended. The smoke, the screaming, his calm certainty. It all added up to something that made no sense.

"I got us out." He didn't look at her, his attention focused on the corridor ahead. "We need to run."

No argument there. Whatever was happening, they needed to get control of her ship. She forced her protesting muscles to move faster, following him through corridors she knew by heart.

The bridge was empty, and there weren't any bodies. Just her violated space with its torn panels and shattered displays. And that broken mug, still in three pieces, mocking her from the floor. She dove for the pilot's seat, hands flying over the controls.

Most of the systems responded, sluggish but functional.

The dock release wouldn't budge.

She tried again. Override codes. Manual disconnect. Every trick she knew.

"They've locked us down." Her fingers cramped as she input another sequence. "We'd need to be on their ship to disengage."

"I will pay for any repairs." He leaned over her shoulder, close enough that she felt his breath on her neck. "Just pull us away."

"You can't pay for repairs if we're dead." She pulled up the structural display, showing him what he was asking. "We'll lose life support and the engines."

The docking mechanism had integrated itself into her hull like a parasite. Ripping free would tear away half her ship's belly, including the primary systems that kept them alive. They'd have minutes at most before the cold of space claimed them.

"Damn it!"

"Exactly." She pushed out of the seat, mind already moving to plan B. "We can try a manual release. If we can access the coupling directly, maybe—"

They ran for the maintenance access, her body

protesting every step. The hatch was already open, tool marks scoring the metal where someone had forced it. She dropped to her knees beside it, peering into the mechanical guts of the connection.

"Definitely black market." She traced the modifications with growing disgust. The coupling had barbed teeth, designed to sink into hull plating and hold on. "This is nasty work. Professional parasite tech."

The mechanism had burrowed into her ship like a tick, barbed connectors making removal impossible without massive damage. Whoever had designed this wanted their prey helpless.

Fighting sounds echoed through the halls, getting closer. Whatever was happening on the pirate ship was spilling over into hers. The hull breach alarm joined the cacophony, its rhythmic shriek making her stomach drop.

"No. No, no, no." She pulled up her wrist display, confirming what the alarm already told her. Pressure dropping in section C. Structural integrity compromised.

This was her ship. Her home. Her freedom. Five years of her life poured into keeping it running, and it was being torn apart by other people's greed. Five years of choosing which meals to skip so she could afford a new regulator. Five years of sleeping in the pilot's seat because the bunk heater was broken and she couldn't afford to fix it.

Five years of her life, bleeding out into the void.

Movement caught her eye. A figure in a dark green space suit rounded the corner, military-grade gear that looked wrong on a pirate. The plasma cannon in their hands was definitely military. Stolen or black market, designed to punch through hull plating like tissue paper.

The barrel swung toward them. Mercy's brain went very quiet, the way it sometimes did when things got truly bad. No time for fear. No time for regrets. Just the simple observation that this was how she died.

She knew this was the end. No dodging plasma. No clever tricks or last-minute escapes. Just super-heated death in a narrow corridor.

The ship rocked violently, something massive impacting the hull. The force flung her sideways, away from Zane. Her shoulder cracked against the bulkhead hard enough to make her vision white out for a second.

The pirate fired. She saw the plasma bloom from the barrel, beautiful and terrible. Her hands came up instinctively, a useless gesture against that kind of death.

Something inside her pulled. Not a physical sensation, not exactly, but something deeper. Like reaching for a door handle in the dark, knowing exactly where it should be. Heat bloomed in front of her, but not the searing agony of plasma.

A wall of fire erupted between her and death. Orange and gold flames that danced and writhed but didn't burn her. They moved like they were alive, like they were listening to something she wasn't saying out loud. The plasma blast hit the barrier and dissipated, its energy absorbed into something greater.

What the fuck?

Then Zane moved. Fire, real fire, erupted from his hands in a torrent that made her little shield look like a candle flame. It roared down the corridor, white-hot at the center, with edges that flickered between orange and blue. The inferno engulfed the pirate, and the scream that followed was mercifully brief. The smell of charred meat and melted plastic filled the corridor.

Silence fell, broken only by the wail of alarms.

Zane stared at her, chest heaving, eyes wide with something that might have been shock. Or fear.

"You control fire?" Her voice came out strangled. Her hands were still raised, and she could see small flames dancing along her fingertips, gold and harmless. But she blinked and then they were gone. How was he doing that? "Since when?"

He took a moment to compose himself, still staring at her like she'd grown a second head. When he spoke, his voice was careful. Controlled. "I'm a dragon."

The words hung between them, simple and impossible. Her brain tried to process this information and came up error. Dragons were myths. Stories. Not real people who complained about wine and made bread in her galley.

"That might have been useful when the fucking pirates started destroying my ship!"

The hull breach alarm shifted from warning to critical. The synthetic voice that followed was calm in the way of machines delivering death sentences. "Structural failure imminent. Abandon ship."

Her anger evaporated, replaced by the cold clarity of survival. Sixty seconds. Not enough time to reach the escape pods. Not enough time to seal the breach. Not enough time for anything but one desperate option.

She and Zane looked at the dock connecting

her dying ship to Horris's vessel. The parasite that had killed her ship might be their only salvation.

"Run." The word came out together, from both of them.

They ran. Through the hatch, across the docking tube that groaned under the pressure differential. Her ship's death screams followed them, metal shrieking as it twisted and tore.

Behind them, the Alto gave one final, shuddering groan, and Mercy felt it in her bones. Five years. Gone.

They burst onto the pirate vessel and straight into Horris's waiting arms.

6

OF ALL THE ships in all the galaxies, Zane had to board hers.

The thought crashed through his mind as Horris's crew surrounded them, weapons drawn and faces hard with the promise of violence. Zane's hands still tingled with residual heat from the fire he'd thrown, his dragon stirring restlessly beneath his skin. The beast wanted blood. Wanted to protect what was his.

His mate.

Mercy.

The realization hit him again, harder this time. She'd redirected his fire. Not dodged it, not shielded herself from it. She'd reached out with some instinct buried deep in her human DNA and turned his flames into a barrier.

The only way that was possible, the only explanation that made any sense at all, was if she was his destined mate.

Fire roared in his veins, begging for release. It would be so easy. A thought, a gesture, and Horris would be ash. His crew would follow seconds later. The ship would be theirs, and he could get Mercy somewhere safe to process what had just happened between them.

"Whatever you're thinking, don't." Horris kept his blaster trained on Mercy's head. The barrel kissed her temple with casual menace. "You're not faster than a plasma bolt."

The pirate captain's scarred face showed no emotion, but Zane could smell the fear beneath his bravado. Good. He should be afraid. If he knew what Zane was thinking, what the dragon wanted to do to anyone who threatened his mate, he'd already be running.

On his left, one of the pirates, a wiry human with nervous hands named Stevn, circled behind him. The man moved like he knew what he was doing, staying out of Zane's peripheral vision.

He needed to focus.

But Mercy stood there with her chin raised and defiance blazing in her eyes, and all he could think about was the way she'd instinctively wielded his fire.

His brothers were going to laugh themselves sick when they found out.

The playboy lord, the one who'd sworn he'd never settle down, undone by a cargo pilot with grease under her fingernails and a tongue sharp enough to flay skin.

Cold metal touched his wrists. The distraction cost him. Stevn had moved while Zane's mind wandered through impossible revelations, and now something sharp pricked his skin. The cuffs clicked shut with finality.

"Try anything funny and those'll fry your brain." Stevn stepped back quickly, like Zane might explode despite the restraints.

Neuro-cuffs. The weight of them was unmistakable, as was the faint electrical hum against his skin. Nasty pieces of technology, designed to scramble neural pathways if the wearer so much as thought about resistance. Usually found in the toolkit of slavers and the worst kind of bounty hunters.

Which told him everything he needed to know about Horris and his crew.

Whatever story they were selling about treasure maps and Mercy's father, their real business involved trafficking people. The modifications to their docking mechanism, the practiced way they'd boarded and searched, the neuro-cuffs ready at hand.

This wasn't their first kidnapping.

His dragon snarled at the thought, but Zane forced it down. The cuffs would detect the spike in aggression, interpret it as hostile intent. He'd seen what the cuffs could do. The screaming had lasted three hours. When it finally stopped, the man had been drooling and vacant, all higher brain function burned away.

No, he needed to be smart about this. Patient. Find a way to get the cuffs off before he made his move.

Horris lowered his weapon, apparently satisfied that the danger had passed. "Take them to the brig and give them some food. We need to get out of here."

The proximity alarms were still wailing, which meant whoever had attacked them earlier might still be in the area. Scavengers drawn by the death of Mercy's ship, maybe. Or legitimate patrols investigating the disturbance.

Stevn grabbed Zane's arm while Krix, a human with facial tattoos that marked him as ex-military, took hold of Mercy. The one who'd searched Zane's quarters and stolen his grandfather's watch. Zane filed that away for later. When this was over, he'd be getting that back, along with several of Krix's teeth.

They marched through corridors that reeked of unwashed bodies and recycled air. The ship was larger than the Alto but in worse repair. Exposed conduits sparked occasionally, and Zane noticed several patches where hull breaches had been hastily welded shut. A faded warning sticker on one bulkhead read "DANGER: EXPLOSIVE DECOMPRESSION" in three languages, but someone had drawn a crude smiley face over it in marker. These people were hanging on by their fingernails, desperate enough to chase legends and kidnap lords.

The brig was exactly what he'd expected. A cage barely large enough for two people, with a narrow bench along one wall and a toilet in the corner that offered zero privacy. The energy field that served as a door hummed with enough power to discourage testing it.

It was, objectively, better than the closet on Mercy's ship. More room to move, to breathe. He was absolutely not stupid enough to say that out loud. Mercy's temper was already balanced on a knife's edge, and comparing their current cell favorably to any part of her destroyed home would end with him bleeding, neuro-cuffs or not.

Krix tossed a single protein pack through the energy field. It hit the floor with a dull thud that somehow made it look even less appetizing than usual.

"Go on then. Fight for it." The tattooed pirate grinned, showing teeth filed to points.

Mercy moved faster than Zane expected, snatching up the protein pack before he'd fully processed the challenge. But instead of keeping it for herself, she broke the bar neatly in half and held out one piece to him.

Their fingers brushed as he took it. The contact sent electricity racing up his arm that had nothing to do with the neuro-cuffs. His dragon surged forward, recognizing its mate through even that brief touch.

Mine, it growled. *Protect. Claim.*

He was completely, utterly fucked.

How had this happened? How had he walked onto a random cargo ship in a cheap port and found the one person in the universe designed for him?

Shade's knowing smile flashed through his memory. The Royal Matchmaker was supposedly psychic, able to see connections others missed. Had she known? Had she orchestrated this somehow?

The protein bar tasted like salted cardboard, but he forced himself to chew and swallow. Mercy needed to see him eating, needed to know he was taking care of himself so she could stop adding his welfare to her list of worries.

When it became clear they weren't going to provide entertainment by fighting over food, Krix and Stevn left. Their footsteps faded down the corridor, leaving Zane and Mercy in relative privacy. As private as you could be in a ship full of pirates who might be monitoring every word.

"What do you mean you're a freaking dragon?" Mercy's voice was harsh. She'd positioned herself on the bench so she could watch the door, ready for threats.

Perhaps he should have mentioned it sooner.

He couldn't tell her about the mate bond. Not yet. Not when she was injured and exhausted and grieving her ship. Not when they were locked in a cage with neuro-cuffs slowly poisoning his system. She needed facts, not more complications.

"I told you I was from Vemion. I'm a dragon lord." He kept his voice as matter-of-fact as possible. Like discussing the weather or navigation routes.

"Honestly, I thought that was just a title." She studied him with those sharp green eyes, cataloging details she'd missed before. "Are you a real dragon, like with scales and everything?"

"When I choose to be."

Her expression shifted through several emotions too quickly to track. Disbelief, wonder, calculation, and finally settling on grim acceptance. Because of course the universe would throw this at her too.

Pirates, treasure maps, and now shapeshifting passengers.

"You did something to the door to get us out." Not a question. She was piecing together the time-line, finding the holes in their captivity.

"I burned a hole in it."

Her gaze flicked to the energy field holding them now, and he could see her doing the math. Wondering why he hadn't already freed them if he had that kind of power at his disposal.

"They're on high alert right now. And I'm not immune to blasters." He shifted, trying to find a position where the neuro-cuffs didn't dig into his wrists. "Right now, they want you. I think you need to give them some hint about this map, to make yourself useful."

"And then we wait for our moment … again?" The skepticism in her voice could have etched glass.

"Exactly."

"We should just take our fucking moment while they're reeling." She stood, pacing the small space like a caged predator. Frustration crackled off her in waves that made his dragon want to growl.

"It may not seem like it, but I have tactical training on how to survive a hostage situation. We need to remain calm." Especially him, or the cuffs might do their worst.

"I am calm." She was absolutely not calm. Her hands clenched and unclenched at her sides, and he could see the moment she registered the blood under her fingernails. Her blood, from wounds she'd taken defending her ship. "You have fire powers. You even used them to protect me from that cannon, didn't you? What's stopping you?"

The question hung between them. He could tell her the truth. That she'd redirected his fire, turned it into something else entirely. That the only person who could do that was someone whose soul was designed to complement his own. That in saving her, he'd found his mate.

But the words wouldn't come. Not here, not like this. She had enough to process without adding an eternal bond to the mix.

He just shrugged. "We need to get these cuffs off me first. Give them what they want, make it seem like we're not a threat, and in a few days, we'll own this ship."

They wouldn't need days. Once he got these cuffs off, once he had a clear shot at Horris without risking Mercy, it would be over in minutes.

She stopped pacing, turned to face him fully. The bruises on her face had darkened to purple-black, and her split lip had started bleeding again. But her eyes were clear, focused.

"Fine. We play it your way. For now." She settled back onto the bench, close enough that their shoulders touched. "But when your moment comes, you better be ready to take it."

He would be. For her, he'd be ready for anything.

7

THE CLEANING RAG in Mercy's hand had seen better days. The synthetic fibers had broken down into something that smeared grime around more than removed it, but she kept scrubbing anyway.

Playing the broken captive meant accepting whatever degrading task they threw at her.

Her knees ached from kneeling on the deck. Her fingers had gone numb from the industrial cleaner that burned through skin as efficiently as it ate through carbon scoring. Every joint in her body protested the repetitive motion, but she kept her head down and worked.

Better this than sitting in that cage with Zane. Better this than thinking about how he'd hidden his true nature while she'd fed him wine and played card games with him.

A dragon.

An actual fire-breathing, shape-shifting dragon who'd played helpless while pirates destroyed her ship.

She attacked a particularly stubborn burn mark with renewed vigor. The longer she spent replaying their time together, the more obvious his act became. The way he'd moved through her galley with super-natural grace. The casual strength when he'd helped secure cargo that should have strained someone of his athletic build. The way he hadn't seemed to get cold, even that night when the ship's heating had been on the fritz and she'd been bundled in three layers.

Not little, her traitorous mind supplied. Nothing about him was little. Not his hands that had covered hers so easily. Not his shoulders that had pressed against hers in that closet. Not the heat that had radiated from his body when they'd been forced together in the dark.

She scrubbed harder.

"You missed a spot."

Horris's voice made her entire body lock up. She forced herself to flinch, to cower back against the wall like a frightened animal. The movement sent pain shooting through her bruised face, reminding her that the fear wasn't entirely an act.

He stood over her, arms crossed, studying her with the same dispassionate interest he might show cargo. She kept her eyes on the deck, counting her breaths. Don't look up. Don't give him a reason.

"Are you ready to talk?"

She wanted to tell him to take his questions and shove them out an airlock. Wanted to spit in his scarred face and accept whatever punishment followed. Her pride demanded it, screaming at her to stand up, to fight, to go down swinging if she was going to go down at all. But Zane's voice echoed in her memory, calm and infuriatingly reasonable.

Make yourself useful. Give them something.

"What do you think I know?" The words came out almost too quietly. Good. Let him think her beaten down, ready to break.

"More than you're telling."

She let silence stretch between them while she scrambled for a story. Something believable. Something that would buy her and Zane time without getting her killed immediately. The trick was making it good enough to be useful but vague enough that they couldn't immediately prove it was bullshit.

"My dad contacted me once a few years ago."

Horris made a sound she couldn't interpret. Not quite interest, but not a dismissal either. "Did he?"

The lie flowed easier than she expected. She let her voice shake, just a little. Let him hear the confusion of a daughter abandoned and suddenly remembered.

"I didn't even realize it was him at first. He didn't look like I remembered him." She almost added details about gray hair or new scars, then caught herself. Horris might know exactly what Rayden Webb looked like now. Might have met him or studied holos, memorized features. Better to stay vague.

"Is he … did you kill him?" She was surprised to realize she actually wanted to know, that somewhere under twenty years of carefully maintained indifference, she'd actually be mad if he had.

Horris snorted. "Never met the man, but I heard he bit it while trying to extract some statuary near ungrateful aliens. They didn't appreciate his work."

Dead. Her father was dead.

The knowledge settled into her chest like a

stone. She waited for grief, for anger, for anything beyond the hollow acknowledgment of fact. But twenty years of abandonment had scoured away whatever feelings might have existed. He'd been a stranger who shared her DNA. Nothing more.

She pushed the non-feelings down deep and focused on the lie. "He didn't give me a map or anything. But he said he was going to the Vacithea Quadrant. That's all he told me."

The place was perfect. Remote enough to be plausible, weird enough to attract treasure hunters, dangerous enough to explain why no one had found anything yet. Stories filtered out of that region regularly. Ghost ships, impossible planets, reality that bent in ways that made navigation computers cry.

Her third year as a pilot, she'd met a woman who swore she'd flown through the Vacithea Quadrant and come out three days before she'd entered. Mercy hadn't believed her, but the woman's ship logs had been convincing enough to buy her drinks for a week.

Horris studied her for a long moment. She kept her eyes down, shoulders hunched, playing the role of defeated prisoner finally breaking under pressure. "That wasn't so hard. Krix, go get our friend some food. I think she's earned it."

The protein ration Krix brought looked margin-ally better than the one from yesterday. She wanted to hide half for Zane, but there was no way to conceal it without being caught. The guards watched her too closely, waiting for any excuse to mete out punishment.

She forced herself to eat it all, hating every bite that didn't go to the man locked in the brig. Hating more that she cared whether a lying dragon lord got fed.

Back to scrubbing. Back to aching knees and burned fingers. She worked her way along the corri-dor, following the trail of carbon scoring from what-ever battle had raged here before they'd arrived. The marks led behind a maintenance partition where ancient life-support equipment hummed and clicked.

She'd just wedged herself into the narrow space when voices approached. Krix and Stevn. She froze, rag still pressed against the wall, suddenly very aware that they couldn't see her behind the machinery.

"I can't believe Mooney's crew caught up to us." Stevn sounded nervous. He always sounded nervous. The man had the constitution of a spooked rabbit. "You think they heard about the girl?"

"Who hasn't these days?"

How? Why? She was nobody—a cargo pilot scraping by on the edges of civilized space, deliberately keeping her head down and her name off any lists that mattered. But apparently, she'd become someone worth hunting.

"But the boss says he's got the biolock from Webb. Her blood's just as good as his."

Krix snorted. "If she's really his kid."

"We tested it. It's a match."

He whistled, low and appreciative. "No shit. Nice."

Her hands started shaking. They'd tested her blood. Really? The thought of them taking samples while she was unconscious, analyzing her DNA without her knowledge, cataloging her genetic markers like she was livestock made bile rise in her throat.

"And she squealed. We're going to unlock the biolock when we get back to base. Three more days until we're millionaires."

"Isn't it a dead-man's lock?" Stevn asked.

"Do you care?"

The cruelty in Krix's voice made her blood run

cold. Everyone knew exactly what extracting a dead-man's biolock meant. It wasn't called that because you needed to be dead to set it up.

It was called that because you had to be dead to open it.

Every drop of blood in her body would be used as a key, drained out slowly while machines analyzed each cell for the genetic markers hidden inside. The process took hours. Sometimes days, if the biolock was particularly complex. You were alive for most of it.

They were going to kill her to try and find her father's treasure.

Someone called their names from farther down the corridor. Their footsteps faded, leaving her alone with the terrible knowledge that she had three days to live.

The rag fell from nerveless fingers. She pressed her back against the wall, legs suddenly unable to hold her weight. Her vision tunneled, black spots dancing at the edges.

Rage replaced fear. Pure, incandescent fury at the universe for this cosmic joke. At her father for making her useful in death when he'd never both-ered to make her useful in life. At Horris and his crew for their greed, for treating murder like a minor inconvenience on the path to profit.

But most of all at Zane and his tactical training and his patient waiting for the perfect moment.

She'd followed his plan, all right. She'd been good and obedient and played the broken prisoner. She'd waited for her moment.

And when they were draining her blood out drop by drop, when she was dying slowly on some filthy med table in a pirate base, she'd make sure he knew exactly how brilliant his advice had been.

8

ZANE SAT on the narrow bench, counting his breaths to keep the neuro-cuffs from detecting his mounting fury. Each inhale brought the stale recycled air that tasted of desperation and decay. Each exhale carried away another fragment of his carefully maintained control.

Mercy had been gone for hours. Cleaning. On her knees, scrubbing floors for pirates who were probably going to murder them.

The cuffs buzzed against his wrists, sensors tracking his neural patterns. One spike of aggression, one moment of lost control, and they'd scramble his brain into soup. He needed to keep his head clear.

He heard footsteps in the corridor, and his head

snapped up. Too light for the guards. Too quick for casual patrol.

Mercy stumbled through the energy field when it dropped, and he took in every new injury in an instant. Scraped knees. Chemical burns on her fingers. Fresh bruises layering over old ones. But it was the expression on her face that made his dragon snarl against its chains.

She was *pissed*.

"These motherfuckers. Fucking assholes!" She whirled on him, green eyes blazing. "And you!"

"Me?" The word came out steadier than he felt. Already, the cuffs were warming, responding to his elevated heartrate.

"Just bide our time, just wait it out." Her voice cracked with bitter fury. "Guess what, Zane, we don't have time."

He forced his breathing to slow, forced his muscles to relax. The dragon wanted to grab her, shake answers from her, then burn the entire ship to ash for whatever had put that look in her eyes. But the cuffs would kill him before he could take a single step.

"What are you talking about?" He kept his voice level, conversational. Like discussing navigation routes over morning coffee. "What's changed?"

She paced the small cell, anger rolling off her in waves that made his skin prickle with awareness.

His mate in distress. His mate threatened.

And him sitting there, useless, trapped by technology designed to break creatures like him.

"I gave Horris some bullshit about my dad, and apparently, that satisfied him." The words tumbled out between ragged breaths. "They have a biolock from my father. A dead-man's biolock."

"What?"

The dragon surged forward before he could stop it. Heat flooded his system, fire racing through his veins. The cuffs sparked, warnings flashing across his vision.

Neural disruption imminent. Compliance required.

She didn't notice his struggle, too lost in her own horror. "It's exactly what it sounds like. They're going to drain every drop of blood from my body to unlock some tech of my fucking dead father's."

No.

The word echoed through every fiber of his being. His mate would not die. Would not be bled dry by greedy pirates chasing legends and treasure. Not while he drew breath. Not while fire still burned in his heart.

The cuffs went from warm to hot. Electricity

danced across his skin, preliminary warnings before the real punishment began. He closed his eyes, reached for every meditation technique his combat instructors had beaten into him.

Center. Breathe. Control.

"We're getting out of here." The words came out rough, barely human. "They won't touch you."

"How?" She stopped pacing, fixed him with those sharp eyes that saw too much. "You're still wearing those cuffs."

He needed to think past the rage, past the dragon demanding blood. Horris wanted treasure. The crew wanted wealth. Greed had always been humanity's most reliable weakness.

"I have a plan."

She studied him for a long moment, then dropped onto the bench beside him. Close enough that her thigh pressed against his, that her scent wrapped around him like silk. Sweat and industrial cleaner and, underneath it all, something that called to the deepest parts of him.

"It better be a good one," she said quietly. "Because I've got maybe seventy hours before they turn me into a blood bank."

Less than three days to get the cuffs off, get her to safety, and preferably leave Horris and his crew as smoking corpses in their wake. His grandfather would have called it a challenge. His brothers would have called it impossible.

Zane called it motivation.

The next morning came too slowly. He spent the night planning, weighing options while Mercy dozed fitfully against his shoulder.

In the morning, after Mercy had been taken away to do more work, the guards brought their usual protein ration, tossing it through the field with casual disdain.

Time to perform.

"You know," he said conversationally, loud enough to carry, "my family would pay quite handsomely for my safe return."

Stevn, the nervous one who'd cuffed him, paused at the field controls. "Sure they would."

"The Vemion Treasury makes most planetary budgets look like pocket change." He shifted, holding up his bound hands with calculated casualness. "The person who ensures my comfort ... who perhaps removes these uncomfortable restraints ... would find themselves very well compensated."

Greed flickered across Stevn's narrow face. Just a flash before suspicion replaced it. "Captain says you stay cuffed."

"The captain isn't here." Zane let aristocratic boredom color his tone. The spoiled lord who'd never been denied anything. "And the captain doesn't need to know about any private arrangements between gentlemen."

"You have no idea what the captain's after."

Perfect opening. Zane allowed himself a small smile. "And you're sure he's going to share it with you? Every credit? Every treasure? Pirates aren't exactly known for their generous profit-sharing."

"Captain's a fair man." The lie was so obvious even Stevn seemed to hear it. His gaze darted toward the corridor, checking for witnesses.

"Even small kindnesses don't go unrewarded," Zane continued. "Extra food, better accommodations. Little things that make captivity more bearable. My family values loyalty, even temporary loyalty. We remember our friends."

Stevn chewed his lip, torn between greed and fear. Greed won, but only partially. He returned with an extra protein ration but kept his hands well away from the cuff controls.

"That's all you get," he muttered, tossing the food through the field. "And don't ask for more."

Progress. Not enough, not nearly enough with time bleeding away, but progress. Zane made a show of grateful appreciation, playing the pampered lord pleased by scraps. Inside, the dragon counted hours.

When evening came, it brought Mercy back to him. She moved stiffly, new exhaustion layering over old. But her eyes held something different. Determination. Purpose. And clutched in her burned fingers, a small piece of metal.

She held it up once the field sealed behind her. A broken tool, narrow and sharp. The kind of thing that littered maintenance corridors on old ships.

"I might be able to destroy the mechanism on those." She nodded toward his cuffs. "I read about it once. But if I mess up—"

"You won't."

"If I do, they'll fry your brain." Her hands trembled slightly, exhaustion or fear or both. "Are you sure about this?"

He was sure about her.

Sure about the fire that had leaped to her command. Sure about the bond singing between them even if she couldn't feel it. Sure that he'd rather die trying to save her than live knowing he'd failed.

"Do it."

She knelt in front of him, taking his hands with

a gentleness that surprised him. This close, he could see every detail. The determined set of her jaw. The way she caught her lower lip between her teeth when concentrating. The steady focus that had kept a dying ship running for years through sheer will.

The metal slipped into the lock mechanism. The cuffs immediately responded, sparks dancing across the surface in warning.

"Hold still," she breathed. "The failsafe is right ... there."

The cuffs went haywire.

Electricity arced between the metal bands, crawling up his arms in burning lines. His vision whited out as the neural scrambler engaged, drilling into his brain with precision agony. This was it. This was how he died. Not in battle, not protecting his mate, but writhing on the floor while his brain melted.

Then silence.

The cuffs fell away, dead metal clattering against the deck. He sucked in air, blinking away the afterimages burned across his retinas. Alive. Whole. Free.

Mercy stared at him, the broken tool still clutched in her hand. "Did I ... are you ..."

He wanted to kiss her. Wanted to pull her

against him and show her exactly what she meant to him, what she'd always meant even before either of them knew it. But they didn't have a second to spare. Guards would come running. They needed to move.

Later. He'd tell her everything later, when they were safe.

Fire erupted from his palm, and he lobbed it at the control panel on the wall. The energy field died with a sharp crack and the acrid smell of burned circuitry. A localized alarm immediately started wailing, but only for the brig.

"Go, go, go!"

They sprinted through corridors, Mercy tugging him one way or another whenever they reached a branching hallway. His fire cleared the path, quick bursts that dropped pirates before they could draw weapons. Mercy snatched a blaster from the first body, covering his back with a competence that made his dragon purr with approval.

His mate was magnificent.

They encountered surprisingly little resistance. Most of the crew was elsewhere, probably counting their future wealth or maintaining the ship. The few pirates they met died too quickly to raise ship-wide alarms.

They burst into the small hangar that held Horris's own luxury short-range transport. Almost all ships of this size had smaller vessels for space to ground travel. It couldn't bounce between systems, and it wouldn't have an FTL drive, but it was *something*.

"Can you fly it?" he asked.

Mercy snorted out a laugh. "I can fly anything."

The certainty in her voice sent heat racing through him that had nothing to do with dragon fire. She meant it. His fierce, impossibly competent mate who could probably pilot a ship with her eyes closed.

The hangar spread before them, Horris's personal shuttle gleaming under harsh work lights. Sleek lines and oversized engines, built for speed rather than cargo capacity. Perfect for running from angry pirates.

Mercy dove for the pilot's seat while he sealed the hangar door with strategic fire. Molten metal was harder to break through than locks. The shuttle's engines roared to life as Zane joined her on the speeder, Mercy's hands dancing across controls like she'd been born to them.

"Hold on," she warned.

The shuttle lurched forward, and the blast door

began to open. Mercy threaded the gap with inches to spare, metal screaming against their hull as they scraped through before anyone could realize they were leaving. Then open space embraced them, stars wheeling past as she pushed the engines hard.

But Horris wasn't done with them yet.

The pirate ship's weapons came online, pulse cannons swiveling to track their escape.

Mercy threw the shuttle into a spiraling dive that made his stomach relocate somewhere around his knees. Plasma fire seared past, close enough to paint their shields with warning lights.

"Where are we going?" she asked, hands never pausing in their dance across the controls.

Good question. They needed somewhere safe, and close. He had no idea where they were or the range of this thing. He needed somewhere he could explain about mates and bonds and everything they could be to one another without her trying to shove him out the airlock.

"I think know a place," he said, and gave her the coordinates.

9

MERCY'S HANDS danced across the controls, muscle memory taking over as another barrage of pulse cannon fire streaked past their starboard side. The shuttle bucked and rolled under her guidance.

She laughed. This was flying.

The pirate ship hung in the viewport behind them, growing smaller by degrees but still very much in weapons range. Their gunners were persistent if nothing else, filling space with deadly light that painted her instruments in warning reds.

She threw the shuttle into a roll that pressed her back into the pilot's seat. G-forces tugged at her bruised face, sent fresh pain shooting through her burned fingers. But pain meant *life*.

"Come on, you piece of garbage," she

murmured to the shuttle. "Show me what you've got."

The engines responded with a throaty roar that vibrated through the deck. Horris kept his personal transport in better shape than his main ship, all right. The coordinates Zane had given her glowed on the navigation display.

Far. Maybe too far for a shuttle's limited range. But she'd nursed dying ships across impossible distances before.

She could do this.

Another volley of plasma fire lit up the void. She rolled left, dove, pulled up hard enough to make her vision gray at the edges. The shuttle protested but held together. Good girl.

The pirate ship fell farther behind. Their weapons fire became sporadic, then ceased entirely as they passed out of effective range. She kept the engines at maximum burn for another ten minutes anyway, putting blessed distance between them and the people who'd wanted her blood.

Only when the proximity sensors showed empty space in all directions did she ease back on the throttle. Her shoulders screamed protest as tension finally released its grip.

"Holy shit, we did it." She turned in her seat to

share the victory with Zane and found him watching her with an expression that stole the words from her throat. He lounged in the co-pilot's chair like he'd been born to occupy the space beside her.

But it was the look in his eyes that made her breath catch. Not the calculated charm of a bored lord. Not the careful mask he'd worn on her ship. This was something else entirely. Something that made heat pool low in her belly despite everything they'd just survived.

His perfect hair had gone wild during their escape. Smoke rose from his shoulders in lazy wisps. And his smile, stars help her, his smile was pure masculine satisfaction. Like a predator who'd successfully defended his territory.

There was a beat of perfect silence between them. His eyes, dancing with impossible flames, dropped to her lips.

How had she ever thought he was anything but a dragon?

Her tongue darted out without conscious thought, wetting suddenly dry lips. The air in the shuttle seemed to thicken, charged with electricity that had nothing to do with damaged systems or firefights. This was older, wild. The recognition of two people who'd been dancing around each other finally running out of reasons to keep their distance.

Rational thought fled.

She reached out and grabbed his collar, expensive fabric bunching under her fingers. One hard pull brought him close enough that she could feel the heat radiating from his skin.

Their lips met, and the universe narrowed to that single point of contact.

She put everything into the kiss. Days of frustration, the terror of almost dying, the fury at his deception, the grudging respect for his competence. But underneath all of that, the truth she'd been avoiding since he'd first walked onto her ship with his lazy smile and ridiculous requests.

She wanted him.

Had wanted him from the moment he'd charmed his way past her defenses with fresh bread and easy conversation. Before she knew about dragons or treasure maps or any of the insanity that followed.

His lips were softer than she'd expected. He claimed her mouth like he had every right to it, with a confidence that made her toes curl in her boots. When she nipped at his lower lip, he groaned against her mouth, the sound reverberating through her chest and settling low in her belly.

His arms came around her, solid and real and radiating heat.

The warmth of him seeped through her clothes, chasing away the lingering chill of space and fear. Every point where their bodies touched sent sparks racing along her nerves. She pressed closer, trying to erase any space between them despite the awkward angle.

The pilot's chair and safety harness conspired against her, keeping her trapped when all she wanted was to climb into his lap and continue this properly.

She angled her head, deepening the kiss, and was rewarded when his hand fisted in her hair. The slight tug sent shivers down her spine. Her lips parted on a gasp, and he took immediate advantage.

His tongue swept into her mouth, and she got her first real taste of him. Something spiced and exotic, with an underlying heat that made her think of cinnamon and flame.

Dangerous.

Addictive.

She made a sound that might have been his

name and felt him shudder in response. The vibration traveled through his chest into hers, and she pressed closer still, desperate to feel more of him.

They broke apart just long enough for her to drag in a shaky breath before he was kissing her again, hungrier this time.

His teeth caught her bottom lip, and she responded by sucking his tongue deeper into her mouth. The wet slide of it against hers was obscene and perfect and made her want to discover what other things he could do with that clever mouth of his.

Her hands found their way to his neck, fingers threading through the hair at his nape. It was softer than it looked, and when she tugged gently, he made a low rumbling sound against her lips. The noise was purely masculine, primal, and it sent heat racing through her veins.

One of his hands found its way under her shirt, calloused palm skating across her ribs before cupping her breast. The first brush of his thumb over her nipple shot electricity straight to her core.

Her back arched involuntarily, pushing herself more firmly into his touch. She moaned into his mouth, wanting more. Needing more. She tugged him closer even as she writhed against the confines of her safety harness. She wanted to touch him everywhere, to map the hard planes of his chest and shoulders with her palms.

She could feel the hard press of his arousal against her hip and nearly whimpered. Knowing that he wanted her just as desperately made her core clench with need. She shifted, trying to create friction, trying to ease the ache building inside her.

It would be graceless and desperate and probably uncomfortable, and she didn't care. She needed …

Zane shifted, trying to get closer, and his elbow slammed into something on the console.

Alarms shrieked through the shuttle. Navigation warnings, collision alerts, a dozen systems protesting whatever he'd accidentally activated. The spell shattered, dropping them back into reality with all the subtlety of a hull breach.

Mercy tore away from him and stared, mouth swollen and wet. Smoke rose from Zane's shoulders in thick plumes now, curling through the recycled air. And his eyes … there was actual fire in them. Not a metaphor, not a trick of light. Real flames dancing in irises, barely contained.

It had to be a dragon thing. Just like the impossible heat of his skin and the way he'd burned through metal and the fact that he'd played her for a fool while she'd served him wine in her doomed galley.

If she said even a single word about wanting more, she knew with absolute certainty that he'd take her right there. Consequences be damned. The hunger in his expression matched her own, magnified by whatever instincts dragons carried in them.

She wanted it so badly she had to bite her tongue to keep the words inside. Wanted his hands on her. Wanted to know what that fire would feel like against bare skin. Wanted to forget about pirates and dead fathers and destroyed ships in the most basic way possible.

But she couldn't. Not now. Not when they were running for their lives in a stolen shuttle with limited supplies and unknown dangers ahead.

She reached over and switched off the alarm with hands that trembled just a bit. The sudden quiet felt too intimate, too heavy with unspoken possibilities.

"You should go check our supplies," she managed, proud when her voice came out steady. Professional. Nothing like the mess of want and confusion churning in her chest. "See if we have any food. We'll be stuck here for a few days."

"Are you sure?" His voice had gone rough, deep in a way that made her insides clench.

She nodded, not trusting herself to speak again. If she opened her mouth, she might beg him to stay. Might throw away the last shreds of her self-preservation and dive headfirst into the thing growing between them.

He hesitated for a moment, studying her with those impossible fire-touched eyes. She could see him fighting the same battle, weighing desire against practicality. Then he stood, moving with that predatory grace she should have recognized from the beginning.

The moment he left the cockpit, she collapsed back against the pilot's seat. Her lips still tingled from his kiss. She could still feel the ghost of his hands on her skin, the hard press of his body against hers.

She was in so much trouble.

Her carefully constructed walls, the ones that had protected her through twenty years of abandonment and loneliness, had crumbled to dust at his touch. All her rules about not trusting charming men, about keeping people at safe distances, about never letting anyone close enough to hurt her, had evaporated.

She'd kissed a dragon. A lying, manipulative, too-handsome-for-his-own-good dragon who'd hidden his true nature while her ship died around them.

And worse, far worse, she wanted to do it again.

She might survive this physically. The pirates were behind them, the shuttle was holding together, and they had a destination. But emotionally?

She was completely, utterly screwed.

10

ZANE WANTED to crawl out of his skin.

The shuttle that had seemed perfectly adequate during their escape now felt so incredibly tiny. Every breath brought Mercy's scent, and it called to his dragon like nothing else ever had. Every shift of his weight reminded him of how she'd felt pressed against him, how perfectly she'd fit in his arms.

He sat in the cargo area, ostensibly checking their supplies but really just trying to put distance between them. The kiss played on endless repeat in his mind. The way she'd grabbed him, fierce and demanding. The little sounds she'd made when he'd touched her. The heat of her mouth and the silk of her skin and the way she'd responded like she was starving for it.

His mate. His brilliant, infuriating, impossible mate who looked at him now like a polite stranger.

Three days of this hell. Three days of careful distance and professional courtesy while his dragon raged against its chains. Three days of watching her pilot the shuttle with the same competence she'd shown flying her own ship, remembering how those clever hands had felt in his hair.

The nav computer chimed their approach to Tonus, and Zane forced himself to focus. The Saffron Court resort spread below them like a jewel against velvet, all golden lights and manicured gardens.

Even from orbit, he could see the careful artistry that went into maintaining the illusion of perfection.

"*That's* where we're going?" Mercy's voice held careful neutrality.

"It'll do."

He bit back a laugh at the irony. This was exactly the kind of place the dissolute failure of a third son would frequent. Expensive enough to impress, seedy enough to find whatever vice you wanted, discreet enough to keep secrets. He'd culti-vated contacts here over the years, playing his role to perfection.

The landing pad materialized from seemingly empty desert, holographic camouflage dropping to reveal pristine metal and waiting staff. Mercy handled the approach with her usual skill, setting them down soft as silk.

"Nice flying."

She shrugged, already powering down systems. "It's what I do."

What she *used to* do. Before pirates destroyed her ship and kidnapped her for blood they thought held treasure maps. Before she'd saved his life by disabling those cuffs with nothing but a broken tool and steady hands.

They unfastened their seatbelts and moved to exit the ship.

Zane had met the security staff a time or two and recognized Myles Judd as he emerged from the resort's discreet entrance. The man moved with the gait of someone accustomed to authority. Silver threads at his temples caught in the light, and his weathered hands rested casually near the blaster at his hip.

Beside him, Mercy's shoulders snapped straight, and her breath caught audibly.

"Judd?"

The man's head snapped up, eyes widening with recognition. "Merc?"

They stared at each other for one suspended moment. The desert wind whipped between them. Then Mercy launched herself down the ramp, and Judd caught her in a hug that lit something acidic and foreign in Zane's chest.

Something was wrong with him.

His vision sharpened to unnatural focus on Judd's hands spanning Mercy's back. His heartbeat thundered in his ears. Heat built beneath his skin, threatening to manifest as flame if he didn't regain control. His fingers curled into fists, knuckles whitening as he fought the urge to stride forward and separate them. The unfamiliar sensation clawed at his ribs like a living thing, demanding action he couldn't name.

Was this some side effect of the neuro-cuffs? Some delayed reaction to the scrambling?

He followed more slowly, trying to identify this bizarre compulsion to separate them. The man was clearly no threat. Just an old friend greeting someone he clearly knew. There was no logical reason for Zane to want to step between them, to remind Judd exactly who had protected Mercy through days of captivity.

No reason at all for this bitter taste in his mouth as he watched them pull apart with matching grins.

His hand moved without conscious thought, reaching out to touch her, to mark his claim in some small way. He caught himself before making contact. His palm tingled with the phantom sensation of her skin, fingers flexing uselessly in the empty air.

She wasn't his. Not yet.

One desperate kiss didn't change that, no matter what his instincts screamed.

"How have you been?" Judd's gaze swept over the stolen cruiser with professional interest. His eyes lingered on the scorch marks along the hull. "Seems you've done well for yourself."

Mercy snorted. "That's a long story." She tucked a strand of hair behind her ear, revealing the bruise that darkened her cheekbone.

That was enough catching up.

"Do you think you can make that disappear quietly?" Zane kept his tone casual as he nodded towards the ship and didn't reach for credits—not that he had any on him. Judd knew payment would be forthcoming. That was how this worked.

Judd blew out a breath through his teeth. "It's a

bit beautiful to go to waste." His fingers traced the shuttle's sleek lines.

"I stripped out the nav tracker," Mercy said, "but there's no telling what else Horris put in there. If you're not opposed to a bunch of pirates chasing you down, it's yours."

"You do live an interesting life." Judd's weathered face creased with amusement.

"Do you have someplace for us to stay?" Zane wanted to be gone. Fast.

"Alma's got you covered." He nodded toward a Kellian woman in a Saffron Court uniform waiting by the entrance.

They followed the woman through corridors that managed to be both opulent and discrete. Soft carpeting muffled their footsteps, and the walls displayed slowly shifting holographic art that responded to their movement with subtle color changes. The air smelled of expensive flowers, nothing like the recycled atmosphere they'd been breathing for days.

Zane barely noticed the decor, but Mercy's head swiveled constantly, taking in the gilt fixtures and hovering light sculptures.

"Nice place," she said.

He shrugged. "I can show you nicer."

She gave him a strange look he couldn't quite interpret.

Alma stopped at a door that looked identical to all the others, pressing her palm to the scanner. The lock disengaged with a soft musical chime, and the door slid open. Behind it was a suite decorated in warm golds and deep reds.

Rich fabrics draped the windows, and plush furniture arranged around a central sitting area invited relaxation. Fresh flowers filled crystal vases, their perfume mixing with the subtle scent of expensive soaps from the bathing chamber. By Saffron Court standards, it was modest. By any other measure, it was luxurious.

"If you need anything, please let us know. As requested, we've provided clothing and other essentials." Alma gestured toward packages arranged on the bedroom's expansive bed, each wrapped in the resort's signature golden fabric.

"Thank you."

She departed with respectful silence, leaving them alone in sudden quiet. Mercy walked through the space like she was cataloging exits and defensive positions.

Then, as if someone had cut her strings, she

collapsed onto a chaise lounge. The fine fabric molded around her frame, and for the first time in days, her shoulders dropped from their defensive hunch.

"I know we have to make plans and stuff, but give me a few minutes," she muttered, face smooshed against fine fabric.

Zane took a chair across from her, indulging in the simple pleasure of watching her exist. Even exhausted, even bruised and burned, she commanded the space around her.

She pushed herself into something that was almost a sitting position. "Do you think I can stay the night before I leave?"

The words hit him like cold water. "What?"

Leave? She wanted to *leave*? They'd just gotten there.

"Is there something wrong here?"

"We're safe. You have to get to Ofros or whatever. I have to …" She seemed to shrink into herself, shoulders curling inward as reality crashed back. Her ship was gone. Her livelihood destroyed. Everything she'd built torn away in a matter of days.

"I'm not going to Ofros." The words came out too sharp, too revealing. He forced himself to relax, to play the careless lord who changed plans on a whim.

She was shaking her head. "You can get transport here; it'll be fine. If I can access my accounts, I can get ... somewhere. Probably I'll need to work on someone's crew and ..." She blew out a breath. "Never mind. You don't care."

Each word was a knife between his ribs. After everything they'd survived together? After she'd risked her life to free him from those cuffs, she thought he didn't *care*?

Remaining calm was getting harder by the second. "We just got here. You don't need to run away so soon."

She gestured at their surroundings. "I can't exactly afford to pay for this room."

"I can."

Her spine straightened, pride flaring in those green eyes. "I took your money for a job I couldn't deliver on, and I can't even give that back. I can't be more in your debt."

"It's not about debt." He leaned forward, willing her to understand. "We both survived. That's what matters."

But he could see her walls solidifying, turning their shared experience into a business transaction gone wrong. His dragon raged against the chains of propriety. He wanted to pull her into his arms and explain exactly who she was to him. Wanted to kiss her until she stopped talking about leaving.

He had a feeling that would make her run away faster.

Instead, he stayed in his chair and scrambled for the right words. "I didn't ever actually want to go to Ofros."

"What?" She turned to face him fully, curiosity momentarily overriding her defensive posture.

"My family wanted me to meet some lady the Royal Matchmaker set me up with." The irony of it nearly choked him. Shade had worked so hard to find him suitable matches, never knowing his mate was flying cargo runs in the outer systems. "I was planning to arrive as my most disreputable self in the hopes that she'd take one look at me and run away."

Mercy stared at him for several beats. Then, unexpectedly, she burst out laughing. The sound filled the suite, bright and genuine and everything he'd been missing since their kiss.

Her eyes tracked over him, slow and considering. "I don't think that would work."

"Why not? It was a brilliant plan!"

The sweep of her gaze felt almost physical, raising heat wherever it lingered. She took in his rumpled clothes, his smoke-darkened hair, the way he filled the delicate chair with barely restrained power. Heat followed in the wake of that gaze, and he had to grip the chair arms to keep from reaching for her.

"I don't think it would be enough to scare away a determined lady."

The moment stretched between them, charged with possibility. He could see her wavering, walls trembling just slightly. Then her expression shuttered, and she looked away. He felt the distance reassert itself like a slap.

Mercy stood abruptly. "I'm going to go wash all this stink off. We can figure out … whatever … later."

He watched her disappear into the bathing chamber, heard the door lock engage with quiet finality. His carefully laid plans, such as they were, crumbled to ash.

He'd thought once they were safe, once they had time, he could find the right way to explain. Could ease her into the truth about … everything.

But she was already planning her escape. Already rebuilding her life without him in it.

He had to find another way. Had to make her see that what sparked between them was more than adrenaline and proximity. Had to convince her to stay long enough to discover what they could be together.

His dragon rumbled with determination. She was his mate. That was immutable, written in fire and blood and the way she'd commanded his flame. But she was also an independent human pilot who'd survived on her own terms.

He just had to figure out how to make her stay.

11

MERCY NEEDED SPACE. And time.

And about a thousand shots of liquor.

Saffron Court was about as far from her life as she could imagine. The decadence pressed against her skin like an ill-fitting suit, making her hyper-aware of every scuff on her boots, every burn on her fingers. Sure, she'd taken vacations before. She'd even dropped passengers at places like this a time or two. But staying at a place like this as a guest?

She felt like someone was going to figure out she didn't belong and throw her out if she held her drink the wrong way.

Zane didn't have that problem. He'd set himself up by one of the luxury pools, fruity drink in hand,

and let himself soak up the sun like this was a vaca-tion and they weren't on the run from a horde of angry pirates.

Her skin was vibrating with worry, and she needed to move.

She wasn't sure if they were in the desert or at the beach. Possibly both. The resort had trans-formed the landscape into something otherworldly, where sand dunes met clear blue water in defiance of natural geography. Water lapped at the edge of the resort, and Mercy walked along, letting the sand squish between her toes.

If she could just live here for about a thousand years, she might be able to relax.

But how much did this place cost? Zane was on a first-name basis with Myles Judd, who was the *head of security* of all things. He'd been little more than hired muscle for a freight hauler when she'd known him a decade ago. But he didn't cheat at cards, and he'd had her back in more than one shady situation.

But it was hard to imagine him in charge of things. He'd been more of a shooter than a thinker when she knew him, with a pile of debt to their shared captain unlikely to ever be paid off.

If this was the kind of place that a dragon lord

went to frequently, it had to be so far out of her price range that she wouldn't even look at it as a joke.

As far as she could tell, Saffron Court owned a large chunk of this planet, maybe the entire thing. There weren't many people around, and those she saw were clearly either guests or staff. All the buildings seemed to be part of the resort, and there wasn't much air traffic.

Under regular circumstances, she couldn't even afford a night.

How could she let Zane pay for this?

Her lips tingled in memory of that kiss. The ghost of his mouth on hers made her stumble slightly in the sand. She could still taste him, could still feel the desperate press of his body against hers in that cramped shuttle cockpit. The sounds he'd made when she'd nipped at his lip, low and rumbling like distant thunder.

She'd wanted to climb into his lap, to forget about pirates and danger and destroyed ships in the most basic way possible. Had wanted it so badly she'd ached with it, every nerve ending screaming for more contact, more heat, more of him.

But she'd pulled back. Because that's what she did. That's what kept her safe.

Except nothing about Zane felt safe. He burned through her defenses like dragon fire through wood, leaving her exposed and wanting things she couldn't afford to want.

Wanting a client had never been an issue before. Usually she hauled cargo, but the few passengers she took on had always remained respectfully professional.

Zane blew past all that without even trying.

And she had no idea who he really was.

Spoiled lord?

Dangerous dragon?

Commitment-phobe?

Maybe all of that. His plan to avoid an unwanted engagement sounded ridiculous, and she had no idea why he couldn't just *talk* to his family about his wants and needs.

Then again, she was walking away from the resort as far and fast as she could to avoid speaking to him, so who was she to say anything?

The water was warmer than she expected, lapping at her ankles with gentle insistence. She found a spot where smooth rock jutted out from the sand, creating a natural seat, and settled down to watch the horizon.

She dug her toes deeper into the sand. This was

real, at least. The grit between her toes, the heat on her shoulders, the ache in her chest that had nothing to do with her recent injuries.

In the distance, she heard the whine of a speeder engine. Common enough at a resort like this. Rich guests needed their toys. She tracked the sound absently, a pilot's habit of monitoring her surroundings, but thought nothing of it until the pitch changed. Growing louder and closer.

Much closer.

Mercy's head snapped up. The speeder was cutting across the beach directly toward her, sand spraying in its wake. Not a leisurely cruise. This was purposeful. Targeted.

Her body moved before her mind caught up, scrambling to her feet and stumbling backward in the soft sand. Her hand reached automatically for a weapon she didn't have. Stupid. She'd gotten comfortable, let her guard down in this paradise of fake beaches and perfect weather.

The speeder skidded to a halt twenty feet away. Two figures in mercenary gear jumped out, their movements too coordinated to be anything but professional. One Kellian with mottled green scales, one human with cybernetic enhancements gleaming at his temples.

"Zane!" she screamed. He was too far away to hear her, she knew that, but her instincts didn't care.

The mercs crossed the distance with deadly efficiency. She tried to dodge, but sand was a terrible surface for quick movements. The human caught her arm, spinning her around while the Kellian produced a handheld scanner. She lashed out with her free hand, catching him across the jaw, but he barely flinched.

"Hold still," the Kellian growled, pressing the scanner to her face despite her struggles. The device beeped, a cheerful sound that made her stomach drop.

"Identity confirmed. Bounty on Mercy Webb in progress." His voice was almost robotic, like he was using some kind of modulator.

Bounty? Her mind raced even as she fought against their grip. Was this Horris's doing? Had he put a price on her head? Or was this something else entirely, some new nightmare connected to her father's legacy?

She drove her heel down on the human's instep, satisfaction flaring when he cursed. But these weren't drunk pirates or station thugs. They moved with military precision, the Kellian producing restraint cuffs while his partner kept her arms pinned.

"Stop fighting," the human said, almost conversationally.

She twisted hard, managing to get one arm free, and clawed at the Kellian's face. Her fingers caught scales, tearing, and he snarled something in his native language.

Brace yourself, she heard Zane's voice in her head and had to be hallucinating. *You're going to be okay.*

A breath later, she heard a dragon's roar loud enough to rattle her eardrums, and a wave of heat rolled over her. Around her. Past her.

But the fire didn't touch her.

What?

The mercs released her instantly, diving away from the inferno that engulfed the space where they'd been standing. Sand turned to glass beneath dragon fire, the heat so intense it warped the air itself. But where Mercy stood, in the center of it all, she felt only warmth. Like standing in sunlight, pleasant and safe.

A massive shadow blocked out the sun. She looked up to see Zane in his full dragon form, wings spread wide enough to darken the entire beach.

Scales caught the light like gold, edged in deep crimson that flickered with inner fire.

He was beautiful. Terrifying. Absolutely magnificent.

The mercs scrambled for their speeder, but Zane wasn't finished. Another blast of fire turned their vehicle into slag, metal running like water into the sand. They tried to run. Pointless. A dragon could cover ground faster than any human, and Zane moved with predatory grace that made her shiver despite the heat.

One more blast of fire, and the mercs were nothing but ash and bone.

Zane landed on the beach with surprising delicacy for something so large, the impact sending tremors through the sand. One massive leg extended toward her, claws carefully tucked away.

Hop on, he said in her mind. *I've got you.*

She might have been going crazy, but right now she would take that over sanity.

His scales were warm beneath her hands, almost hot, but not burning. She found purchase between the larger plates, hauling herself up with muscles that remembered climbing cargo nets and access ladders. It should have been terrifying, clinging to a creature out of legend.

It wasn't.

The world dropped away as he launched skyward. Wind whipped at her hair, tore at her clothes, but she pressed close to his neck and held on. Below them, the resort sparkled, and she could see the dark spots on the beach where sand had turned to glass.

Evidence of dragon fire. Evidence of Zane's protection.

They circled back to their suite, Zane hovering with remarkable control beside their balcony. She slid off carefully, her legs shaky as they hit solid ground. Then she watched, transfixed, as he transformed mid-air. The massive dragon form condensed, shifted, reformed into the man she knew. He landed on the balcony with casual grace, as if shape-shifting in mid-air was perfectly normal.

Wow.

His face was a mask of fury as he ushered her inside. Smoke was coming off of his body in waves, making their room smell a bit like a campfire.

"I'm alright," she told him. She placed her hand on his arm, and he froze. Beneath her palm, his skin radiated heat like a furnace, and she could feel the tremor of barely controlled rage running through him. "How did you do that? Not burn me up?" If she thought about it too hard, she might go crazy, so she was trying to remain calm. Logical. As if logic was possible at a time like this.

He huffed for a moment until his breathing evened out. "I was careful." But it felt like he wasn't saying something.

What wasn't he saying?

"What kind of shitshow is Judd running?" Zane growled. His hands clenched and unclenched at his sides, and she could see the effort it took not to punch something. "This place is supposed to be *safe*."

"They said something about a bounty. They scanned my face and confirmed my identity. It wasn't a mistake."

Fresh smoke curled from his shoulders, and his eyes flickered with actual flames. The temperature in the room jumped several degrees. "I'm going to kill them for touching you."

"I think you already did that."

"Not enough." The words came out more growl than speech. He paced the suite like a caged predator, every movement sharp with barely leashed violence. "They put their hands on you. Threatened you. I should have—"

"You saved me." She kept her voice steady,

soothing. Like talking to a spooked beast, except this particular beast could breathe fire. "That's what matters."

He stopped pacing, fixing her with those impossible eyes. The fury was still there, but underneath it, something else. Something that made her chest tight and her pulse skip.

They stood there for a moment. Then Zane seemed to pull himself together, the smoke dissipating as he regained control. He moved to the sofa, and after a beat, she joined him. Not touching, but close enough that she could feel his warmth.

"We need to tell Myles," said Mercy.

Zane grumbled when she said that name. Strange. "I'm sure he knows by now."

The adrenaline was fading, leaving her shaky and too aware of everything. Of how Zane's shirt stretched across his shoulders. Of the way his jaw tensed when he was thinking. Of how he'd roared her name across a beach and turned her attackers to ash without hesitation.

She'd never had anyone protect her like that. Never had anyone care enough to come running when she screamed. It was terrifying and wonderful and made her want things she couldn't have.

Because men like Zane didn't stay. They played

hero for a while, enjoyed the thrill, then went back to their real lives. Their important lives that didn't include broke cargo pilots with more baggage than credits.

But the way he was looking at her now ...

"Come home to Vemion with me," he said suddenly. "I can keep you safe there. No one will touch you."

"That's a nice offer, but from the sounds of it, no one would like it if you showed up with ... me when you're supposed to be finding your own lady." She had to shut it down before she dared let herself dream.

His eyes flashed, and for a moment, she saw dragon fire in their depths. "I don't give a damn about that. Come with me. Let me protect you. Let me ..." If he was going to say more, he thought better of it and trailed off.

Mercy wasn't sure how she was supposed to take that. It didn't sound like he was talking short term. It sounded like ... she couldn't let herself think about what it sounded like.

Because thinking about it would mean acknowledging the way her heart hammered when he looked at her. Would mean admitting that when he'd spoken in her mind, it hadn't felt foreign or wrong or like some sort of hallucination.

It would mean accepting that she wanted to say yes. Wanted to follow this impossible dragon lord to his impossible world and let him keep her safe. Let him keep her.

This was insane. They'd known each other less than a week. Most of that time was spent running for their lives. She didn't do this. Didn't want people like this, with a desperation that clawed at her ribs and made rational thought impossible.

But when had anything about Zane been rational?

She crossed the couch and kissed him.

12

MERCY'S LIPS crashed against Zane's with all the desperation of a drowning woman finally finding air.

She tackled him back against the couch cushions, her hands fisting in his shirt as she straddled his lap. The kiss was messy, urgent, nothing like before. This was need and fear and relief all tangled together, pouring out through the press of her mouth against his.

He tasted like danger wrapped in silk. His lips were soft, but his kiss was anything but gentle. When she nipped at his bottom lip, he groaned deep in his chest, the sound vibrating through her entire body where they pressed together. Heat radiated from his skin, not quite human warmth but something fiercer, more elemental.

Dragon heat. The heat that had turned her attackers to ash but left her untouched.

Her mind reeled, trying to process the impossible duality of him. This man, who baked bread and played cards with her, who cleaned her galley until it sparkled. The same man who could transform into a creature of legend and rain fire from the sky.

But right now, with his arms wrapped around her and his mouth moving against hers, he felt like he was all hers.

Zane's hands tangled in her hair, angling her head to deepen the kiss. His tongue swept into her mouth, claiming and exploring, and she moaned against him. Fire raced through her veins, pooling low in her belly. Every nerve ending sparked to life, her body going liquid with want. She needed more. Needed to feel him, all of him, needed to confirm he was real and solid and *here*.

Her hands traced over his shoulders, mapping the broad expanse through expensive fabric. Muscle shifted beneath her palms, coiled strength that had carried her to safety. She could feel the power thrumming just beneath his skin, barely leashed.

No one had ever come for her before.

The thought made her kiss him harder, pouring all her confusion and gratitude and want into the connection. Her fingers found the hem of his shirt, tugging impatiently. She needed skin. Needed to feel the heat of him without barriers.

Zane pulled back just enough to look at her, and she gasped. There was literal fire dancing in his eyes, flames flickering in brown irises like embers in a hearth. Another reminder that he was more than human, more than she could fully comprehend.

But she didn't care. Not now. Not when her body was singing with need and her heart was still racing from terror and rescue and the impossible fact that she was alive.

Her hands shook as she pulled at his shirt, fumbling with fabric that suddenly seemed far too complicated. She needed to touch him, needed to confirm he was real and whole and *here*. That they'd both survived. That those mercs hadn't dragged her away to whatever fate awaited girls with bounties on their heads.

"Easy," he murmured, his voice rough with barely controlled want. His hands covered hers, steadying them. Together, they worked his shirt over his head, and then her palms were finally, finally on his bare skin.

He burned like a furnace, heat radiating from every inch of exposed flesh. Her hands mapped the planes of his chest, feeling the way his muscles tensed beneath her touch. Scars marked his skin here and there, thin white lines that spoke of a life less pampered than she'd assumed. Her fingers traced each one, learning this new landscape of him.

"I need to see you," he said, and his hands were gentle as they found the hem of her shirt. So different from the rough grip of the mercs, the violence of being grabbed and scanned like cargo. Zane's touch was reverent, careful, giving her every opportunity to pull away.

She didn't want to pull away. She wanted to fall into him and never surface.

Her shirt joined his on the floor, and then his hands were on her skin, warm and sure. He traced the bruises on her ribs with heartbreaking gentleness, the chemical burns on her fingers, the scrapes from her time with the pirates. Each touch felt like an apology, a promise, a claim all rolled into one.

When his mouth followed his hands, pressing kisses to each injury, she thought she might shatter.

No one had ever touched her with such care. Like she was precious. Like she mattered.

"Beautiful," he murmured against her skin, and she believed him. In this moment, with his hands and mouth worshipping every inch of her, she felt beautiful. Felt wanted.

The rest of their clothes disappeared in a blur of desperate hands and tangled limbs. She needed to feel all of him against all of her, skin to skin with nothing between them. When they were finally bare, she pressed against him with a soft cry of relief. The heat of him chased away the lingering cold of fear, warming her from the outside in.

He was magnificent.

All lean muscle and controlled power, strength that could level buildings channeled into gentle touches. Her hands couldn't stop moving, needing to touch and claim and confirm. This impossible man who was hers, at least for now.

At least for this moment stolen from chaos.

"Let me," he said, and she wasn't sure what he was asking but she nodded anyway. Trust, she realized with a start. She trusted him. This dragon who'd hidden his nature, who'd saved her life, who looked at her like she hung the stars.

His mouth traced a path down her body, and

she surrendered to sensation. Let herself stop thinking, stop analyzing, stop planning for once in her life. There was only feeling as he mapped her with lips and tongue and careful teeth.

Only the building pressure as he found every sensitive spot and lavished it with attention.

When his mouth finally found her center, she arched off the couch with a cry. Pleasure sparked through her like lightning, sharp and bright and overwhelming. Her hands fisted in his hair, holding on as he took her apart with focused intensity. The vulnerability of it should have terrified her.

But this was Zane. Zane, who'd burned for her, flown for her, offered her sanctuary without asking for anything in return. She could be vulnerable with him. Could let down her walls and just *feel*.

The pressure built and built until she shattered with his name on her lips. Waves of pleasure crashed over her, leaving her boneless and gasping. He worked her through it, gentle now, until she tugged at his hair to bring him back up to her.

His eyes still held traces of fire as he looked at her, and she could feel the hard length of him pressed against her thigh. Ready. Waiting. Letting her decide what came next even though she could see the strain of holding back written across his features.

She pulled him down for a kiss, tasting herself on his lips. "Please," she whispered against his mouth. "I need you."

The words were inadequate for what she actually needed. Not just his body, though she craved that with an intensity that surprised her. She needed the connection, the affirmation of life after facing death. Needed to feel claimed and cherished and whole.

He entered her slowly, carefully. The stretch and fill of him made her gasp, her body adjusting to the intrusion. But it was good, so good, like coming home to a place she'd never known she'd been searching for.

"Perfect," he growled, and there was something inhuman in the sound. "You feel perfect."

She couldn't form words to respond, too lost in sensation. He filled her completely, the heat of him warming her from within. When he started to move, slow and deep, she wrapped her legs around his waist and held on.

This was nothing like her previous experience. This was connection on a level she didn't have words for. Every thrust felt like a claim, every kiss a promise. Her body sang with rightness, like this was what she'd been made for.

This man, this moment, this impossible feeling of belonging.

His control started to slip as they moved together. She could see it in the way his eyes flickered with flame, hear it in the growls that rumbled from his chest. His skin grew hotter, almost burning, but it didn't hurt. It felt like being wrapped in safety, in power, in something ancient and unbreakable.

"Mine," he growled against her throat, and she should have bristled at the possessiveness. Should have reminded him that she belonged to no one. Instead, she found herself arching into him, baring her throat in submission.

"God, yes," she gasped, and felt him shudder against her.

The pressure built again, spiraling higher with each thrust. She was close, so close, balanced on the edge of something vast and terrifying and wonderful. Then Zane's hand found the place where they were joined, his thumb circling with just enough pressure, and she flew apart.

This climax hit harder than the first, stealing her breath and her thoughts and possibly her sanity. She clung to him as pleasure whited out her vision, her body clenching around him. She felt him follow her over, his own release pulled from him with a roar that was definitely more dragon than man.

They collapsed together on the couch, sweat cooling on their skin. Mercy's mind felt blissfully quiet for the first time in days.

No plans, no fears, no constant calculation of threats and exits. Just the warm weight of Zane's body covering hers, the steady thrum of his heartbeat against her chest.

She should move. Should retreat to the bathroom and rebuild her walls and pretend this was just physical release after trauma. Should do anything but burrow closer into his embrace and let herself feel safe.

But she was so tired of running. Tired of being strong and independent and alone. Just for tonight, just for this stolen moment, she could let someone else be strong for her. Let someone else stand guard while she rested.

She let herself rest against Zane and pretended everything would be alright.

13

ZANE HELD Mercy against his chest, feeling the rapid flutter of her heartbeat gradually slow to match his own. Her hair tickled his chin, dark strands still damp with sweat, and he resisted the urge to bury his face in it and breathe her in. Every instinct screamed at him to wrap her up, carry her somewhere safe, and never let her out of his sight again.

His mate. Finally in his arms where she belonged.

Time was slipping away, and he could feel her starting to think again. Her muscles tensed slightly against him, the first sign that her walls were rebuilding. Soon, she'd find some excuse to put distance between them. Then she'd start talking about leaving again, about finding work on someone else's crew.

He couldn't let that happen. Not when he'd finally found what he hadn't even known he was looking for.

Mercy's fingers traced lazy patterns across his chest, following the lines of muscle and the thin scars he'd accumulated over the years. Her touch was gentle, almost reverent, like she was memorizing the feel of him. The sensation sent warmth racing through his veins that had nothing to do with dragon fire.

"You really were going to sabotage some matchmaking meeting?" Her voice held amused disbelief. She tilted her head to look up at him, green eyes still soft with satisfaction but sharpening with curiosity. "Not that I'm complaining, but it seems a bit extreme. Why not just say no?"

How could he explain it without sounding like the spoiled lord she'd initially assumed he was?

"I'm the youngest of three, did you know that?" He kept his tone light, conversational, even as his hand found its way into her hair.

"That's one of the least surprising things I've heard."

The dry delivery made him laugh despite his

nerves. Trust Mercy to cut straight through any attempt at sympathy. He growled playfully and rolled them both, pinning her beneath him on the wide couch. Her startled laugh turned into a gasp as he captured her mouth in a quick kiss, nipping at her lower lip until she squirmed against him.

"Okay, I surrender!" She was breathless when he finally pulled away, her cheeks flushed and eyes bright with laughter. "You're the poor, abused youngest brother who was being forced to marry some poor woman to secure your inheritance, is that it?"

"Not exactly." The assumption stung more than it should have. He didn't want her thinking he was some penniless younger son trading his title for financial security. Money had never been an issue for any of his family. "I'm not poor."

"Well?" She traced her fingers along his jaw, the simple touch making it hard to concentrate on words. "What's the real story then?"

He settled back beside her, pulling her against his side where she fit like she'd been made for the space. Outside, the resort's evening entertainment was beginning. Soft music drifted up from the pools below, mixing with distant laughter and the gentle splash of water.

"My brothers, Rook and Vex, just found their mates. One right after the other, as if by magic." He couldn't keep the snort of disbelief from his voice. The timing had been absurd, both of them falling head over heels within weeks of each other.

And now here he was …

He had to press on.

Mercy gave him a look that was equal parts amused and incredulous. "You're a dragon and you don't believe in magic?"

Okay, fair point. He breathed fire and could transform into a creature of legend, yet he'd always approached life with cold logic. Maybe that was part of his problem.

"I believe in the here and now." The words came out softer than he'd intended. The here and now was Mercy, warm and willing in his arms. The rest could wait.

She studied his face for a moment, something flickering in her eyes before she looked away. "Go on. About your brothers."

Right. The explanation she deserved. "Anyway, my family decided it was time for me to end my ne'er-do-well ways and settle down. They arranged this meeting with the Royal Matchmaker. I couldn't say no."

"Why not?" Her fingers had found their way back to his chest, tracing idle patterns that made it difficult to focus on anything else.

This was the part that made him sound like exactly the privileged lord she'd initially pegged him as. But she'd asked, and he owed her honesty.

"It's difficult to say no to your uncle. Especially when he's the king."

Mercy went very still against him. Her hand froze mid-motion, palm flat against his ribs. He could practically hear her mind working, putting together pieces she hadn't had before.

"Your uncle is the king," she repeated slowly. "Of dragons."

"Well, of Vemion, but yes."

"Which makes you …"

"Somewhere in line for the throne, technically. Though it's not something I think about much." The succession had never mattered to him. He had plenty of cousins in line ahead of him. He'd been content to play the useless younger brother, free to pursue his own interests without the weight of expectation.

Until now. Until her.

She sat up abruptly, the sheet pooling around

her waist as she stared at him. "You're royalty. Actual royalty."

"Dragon lord, but yes, technically." He reached for her, wanting to pull her back down beside him, but she evaded his grasp.

"And you were on my cargo ship why, exactly?" Her voice had gone carefully neutral, the way it did when she was processing something she didn't like.

This was going wrong. He'd told her part of it before, but now he owed her a bigger, *real* explanation.

"I thought if I showed up in transport not fit for a lord … not that your ship wasn't wonderful …" He caught her hand before she could retreat further, pressing her palm back against his chest. "And played my most rakish self, whatever lady the Matchmaker found for me would run screaming."

Mercy's expression was unreadable. She didn't pull away, but she didn't relax either. "I see. And what are you going to do when we get out of this mess?"

The question hit him hard. She was already planning their separation, already thinking past whatever this was between them. As if what they'd just shared was nothing more than stress relief, a pleasant interlude before returning to their separate lives.

"I'm not looking for someone else."

The words came out more intense than he'd intended, weighted with everything he didn't know how to say. About the way his dragon had recognized her from the first moment. About how her fire had answered his call.

She studied his face, searching for something he hoped she could find. Her green eyes held wariness now, the same caution she'd shown when he'd first walked onto her ship. Like she was waiting for the catch, the moment when he'd reveal this was all some elaborate game.

"Mercy." He shifted to face her fully, taking both her hands in his. They were still marked with injuries from the pirates, still callused from years of hard work. Beautiful hands that had saved his life, that had touched him with such reverence. "I've been running from commitment my entire life. From duty, from expectations, from anything that felt like a cage."

Her breath caught slightly, but she didn't speak.

"I don't want to run from this." He lifted one of her hands to his lips, pressing a soft kiss to her knuckles. "From you. What we have … it's different. It feels …"

"Feels what?" The question was barely a whisper.

"Right." The word was inadequate for what he actually meant. Destined. Inevitable. Written in fire and stars and the very fabric of the universe. But he couldn't say that without sounding insane. "Like I've been looking for you my whole life without knowing it."

The irony wasn't lost on him. His elaborate plan to avoid finding a bride had led him directly to his mate. He'd boarded her ship intending to play the dissolute failure and instead found the one person who saw through every mask he wore. Who called him on his lies and saved his life and commanded his fire like she'd been born to it.

"Zane …" Her voice held warning, but also something else. Hope, maybe. Or fear. Possibly both.

"Come to Vemion with me." He tightened his grip on her hands, willing her to understand. "Not just for safety. Because I want to be with you. I want to see what we could build together."

It was a risk. He was asking her to leave everything she knew, to trust him with her future. To take a chance on something that defied logic and probability and everything her hard life had taught her about self-preservation.

But instead of answering, instead of the careful analysis he expected, she leaned forward and kissed him.

This kiss was different from the desperate claiming that had started this. Softer, deeper, weighted with decision and acceptance and something that might have been surrender. She poured herself into it, and he tasted possibility on her lips. Tasted yes.

His arms came around her, pulling her against him. Her hands fisted in his hair, holding him close, and he could feel the exact moment her walls crumbled. The moment she stopped fighting what was between them and let herself fall.

They made love again as the sun set outside their windows, slower this time, savoring each touch and kiss and whispered endearment. He worshipped her body with his hands and mouth, memorizing every curve and hollow, every sound she made when he found a particularly sensitive spot.

When she finally took him inside her again, it felt like coming home.

Afterward, as they lay tangled together, Zane allowed himself to hope. She hadn't said yes in words, but her body had given him an answer. Her kiss had tasted like acceptance, like trust, like the beginning of forever.

His mate was in his arms, safe and willing and his.

It had to be enough.

14

MERCY HAD BEEN awake for nearly an hour, listening to Zane's steady heartbeat and trying to make sense of the tangle of emotions in her chest.

Everything felt different now. The careful walls she'd built over twenty years of abandonment and disappointment had crumbled under his touch. The independent cargo pilot who trusted no one had melted into someone who wanted impossible things. Someone who was seriously considering following a dragon lord to his homeworld based on nothing more than the way he kissed her and the promise in his eyes.

It was terrifying.

"I can hear you thinking," Zane murmured against her hair, his voice rough with sleep. His arm tightened around her, pulling her closer to the furnace of his body.

"I need to go see Myles." She lifted her head to look at him, noting the way his jaw tensed at the other man's name. "About the bounty and the attack. To figure out what our options are."

"I'll come with you."

The immediate response made warmth flutter in her chest, even as her independence bristled. "I need to do this alone. He's an old friend. He might be more willing to help if it's just me."

Zane's eyes flickered with something that might have been dragon fire. The possessive streak that had emerged yesterday was still there, barely leashed. "After what happened on the beach?"

"This is different. Myles has known me for years. He's not going to hurt me." She pressed her palm against his chest, feeling the rapid thrum of his heartbeat. "I can handle this myself. You understand that, right?"

The internal struggle played out across his features. The dragon that wanted to wrap her up and keep her safe warred with the man who respected her competence. Finally, he nodded, though she could see the effort it took.

"If you're not back in two hours, I'm coming after you."

"Deal." She leaned down to kiss him, meaning it to be quick and reassuring. But the moment their lips met, heat flared between them. His hand fisted in her hair, deepening the kiss until she was breathless and aching all over again. When they finally broke apart, his eyes held flecks of fire that hadn't been there before.

"Be careful," he said, and the rough edge to his voice made her shiver.

She had to escape the room before another kiss could turn into something more.

She found Myles near the hangar where they'd landed the stolen shuttle. The morning sun cast long shadows across the landing platform, and maintenance crews moved with purpose around various aircraft. The shuttle was gone. Probably already stripped for parts or sold to someone who wouldn't ask inconvenient questions.

"Merc!" Myles straightened from where he'd been examining a sleek transport, his weathered face creasing into a smile. "How are you holding up?"

"I've been better." She fell into step beside him

as he continued his inspection route. "We need to talk about what happened yesterday."

"I heard." His expression sobered. "Bad business, that. How many bodies do you think I can clean up?"

"If I knew that, I'd tell you." She kicked at a piece of debris, watching it skitter across the polished platform. "We escaped from a pirate calling himself Horris. He had some … strange ideas about me and my dad."

Myles nodded thoughtfully. His comm unit chirped, and he held up a finger before answering. "Judd here. What? No, tell them to wait. I'll be ready in an hour or so." He ended the call with an apologetic shrug. "Sorry. Where were we?"

"Figuring out how screwed I am."

"You know, I have to say I'm surprised." Myles resumed walking, hands clasped behind his back in a gesture she remembered from their freight-running days. "I didn't really think you were Zane's type. Or that he's yours."

Something in his tone made her stomach clench. "What do you mean?"

"Well, he's got quite the reputation. Did you know he once fled from Lady Persoff's bedroom wearing nothing but a bedsheet? Had to scramble down three stories of castle wall while her husband chased him with a plasma sword."

The words hit her like ice water. "What?"

"Oh, that's nothing compared to the Pinae incident." Myles laughed, apparently oblivious to her shock. "He seduced three of their sacred courtesans right out from under Emperor Zil's nose. Had to be smuggled off-planet in a cargo container when they put a death mark on him."

Mercy's mind reeled. The man who'd baked her bread and cleaned her galley? The one who'd held her like she was precious? "Are you sure we're talking about the same person?"

"Dragon lord Zane of Vemion?" Myles's eyebrows rose. "Trust me, his exploits are legendary. Half the noble houses in three systems have banned him from their social functions. The other half are just waiting for their chance."

Each word was a knife between her ribs. She thought of how Zane had kissed her, like he wanted forever. How he'd asked her to come to Vemion, to build something together. Had it all been an act? Another conquest for the notorious playboy prince?

"I had no idea," she managed. He'd talked about avoiding the Matchmaker, about not wanting attachment. But hearing actual stories rather than whatever he'd implied …

Could he mean it when he looked at her like things were real? Was that how he'd looked that the courtesans?

"Don't take it personally. He's charming as hell when he wants to be. Just don't expect anything permanent. Commitment isn't exactly his strong suit."

Myles said more, but Mercy barely heard it. Her thoughts spun in sickening circles, replaying every moment with Zane through this new lens. Had he been laughing at her naivety? The independent pilot who'd fallen for the oldest trick in the book?

"Listen," Myles said, and she forced herself to focus. "I can get you out of here safely. I still have contacts with some decent crews who could use a good pilot. You could work your way back up to your own ship again."

Her old life. The one where she answered to no one, trusted no one, needed no one. It should have sounded like salvation. Instead, it felt hollow.

"You could have your life back, Merc. The way it was before all this pirate nonsense."

But did she *want* her life back?

The loneliness, the constant struggle, the walls that kept everyone at arm's length? Even if everything Myles said about Zane was true, even if she'd been a fool to trust him, going back to that existence felt like a kind of death.

"Why don't you think it over?" Myles suggested. "You can use my office. Get away from any distractions and really consider your options."

Distractions. Meaning Zane. The man who might have been playing her from the beginning.

Or who was offering her everything and ready to give up his playboy life for … her.

She nodded numbly and followed Myles to a modest office tucked away from the guest areas. It was a standard administrative space with a desk, chair, and single window overlooking the landing platforms.

"Take all the time you need," Myles said, closing the door behind him.

Mercy slumped into the chair, her head in her hands. The stories Myles had told painted a picture of a man nothing like the one she'd come to know. But which version was real?

The commitment-phobic playboy or the gentle dragon who'd held her through the night?

She thought about their conversations,

searching for signs she'd missed. The way he'd talked about running from duty and expectations. His plan to sabotage the matchmaking meeting. Even his offer for her to come to Vemion, was that just another game? Another challenge to overcome?

But then there was the other stuff. The way he'd looked at her when he thought she wasn't watching. The protective fury when the mercs had grabbed her. The reverent way he'd touched her injuries, like each one caused him physical pain.

The way he'd killed for her.

Whatever else Zane might be, whatever his past looked like, that moment on the beach had been real. The connection between them was real.

And Myles was full of shit. Maybe the stories were true, but that wasn't Zane, not anymore.

She stood abruptly. She was done running from things that scared her. Done letting other people's opinions dictate her choices. Zane had a past. So did she. Maybe he'd made mistakes. But she'd felt something real between them, and she was willing to fight for it.

And she wasn't going to let Myles talk her out of anything.

She was ready to go find Zane and tell him exactly that. But the door handle didn't turn.

She tried again, putting her shoulder into it. Nothing. The mechanism didn't even click.

"What the hell?" She examined the lock, but it was a standard electronic system. No manual override she could see. "Myles!"

No response.

Had he *locked* her in?

Her mind was reeling with questions when she heard a transport shuttle's engines roar to life outside. She turned to the window, watching as a familiar ship settled onto the landing platform. Her blood turned to ice as it powered down and the hatch slid open.

Horris stepped out.

Even from a distance, the pirate captain looked exactly as she remembered. Bulky frame, scarred face, the casual arrogance of a man accustomed to taking what he wanted. He scanned the platform like he owned it, then smiled as Myles approached.

They shook hands like old friends.

What the ever-living *fuck?*

Devastating betrayal roiled through her. Myles hadn't been protecting her. He'd been *stalling*. Keeping her distracted while he waited for Horris. The comm call, the stories about Zane, the offer to help her escape, all of it had been theater.

Her old friend had sold her out.

Had he done it before or after those mercs had found her on the beach? Had that tipped him off? Or had she done it herself when they landed and told him the whole sordid tale?

She watched through the window as credits changed hands. Watched Myles point toward the building where she was trapped. Watched Horris nod and gesture to his crew.

They were coming for her.

Mercy pressed her back against the door, mind racing. She had to get out of there. Somehow. She didn't have a comm unit, and there wasn't a built-in one on the desk. She tested the window, but it didn't open.

If—no, *when*—she lived through this, she wasn't going without a weapon ever again.

She banged on the door and tried to kick the lock. It did nothing.

Outside, Horris and his crew were already moving toward the building. In minutes, they'd be at the door. In hours, she'd be back in that cramped cell, counting down to her death.

She'd trusted the wrong person. And she was going to die for it.

15

SOMETHING WAS WRONG.

Zane stood at the suite's window, watching the morning light play across the resort's pristine grounds. Mercy had been gone for over an hour. Long enough for a simple conversation about bounties and security protocols. Long enough for his dragon to start pacing restlessly beneath his skin.

He told himself he was being paranoid. She'd said Myles was an old friend, someone she trusted. And he'd known Judd long enough to know he was a competent man. She'd asked for space to handle things herself, and he needed to respect that. Crowding his mate would only send her running back to the independent life she'd built for herself.

But every instinct he possessed screamed that something was *off*.

The rational part of his mind provided perfectly logical explanations. Myles could have been called away on resort business. Mercy might have gotten distracted by the technical specs of some new ship in the hangar. She could be catching up with her friend over coffee, sharing stories about their freight-running days.

His dragon didn't care about logic. His dragon was certain his mate was in danger.

His dragon needed to get a grip.

Zane ran both hands through his hair, trying to settle the restless energy building under his skin. Already, smoke was pouring off of him, making the room smell like a campfire.

He was new to this whole mating thing. Maybe protective paranoia was normal. Maybe every dragon lord spent the first few weeks after finding their mate jumping at shadows and imagining threats that didn't exist.

But Mercy's scent was fading from the suite, and his skin itched with the need to find her. To confirm she was safe with his own eyes.

Ten more minutes. He'd give her ten more minutes, then he'd go looking. He could apologize for intruding on her privacy later. Somehow. Maybe with a nice bottle of wine and a massage.

He'd told her she had two hours. What was a few dozen minutes difference?

The minutes crawled by like hours. Outside, resort staff moved through their morning routines. Guests lounged by pools that sparkled like jewels in the desert sun. Everything looked perfectly normal.

So why did the hair on the back of his neck refuse to settle?

Eight minutes left.

He paced the suite's main room. The space felt too large without Mercy's presence, too empty despite the luxury furnishings. Her clothes from yesterday lay draped over a chair where she'd left them, and he caught himself breathing in the faint trace of her scent that clung to the fabric.

Pathetic. He was acting like a lovesick teenager instead of a grown dragon lord with generations of breeding behind him.

Five minutes.

The comm unit on the side table chimed softly. Zane lunged for it, hoping for a message from Mercy explaining the delay. Instead, he found a routine notification about meal service and entertainment schedules. Nothing useful.

His reflection in the darkened screen showed wild hair and eyes that flickered with barely contained fire. He looked like exactly what he was. A dragon whose mate was out of sight and potentially in danger.

Three minutes.

To hell with it.

Zane grabbed a shirt and headed for the door. Mercy could scold him for being overprotective later, preferably while she was safe in his arms. Right now, he needed to see her. Needed to confirm his instincts were wrong and she was perfectly fine.

The resort was easy enough to navigate. He'd visited Saffron Court often enough over the years to know the layout. Myles Judd's office was tucked away in the administrative wing, a modest space that reflected the man's practical nature.

The door stood slightly ajar when Zane reached it. No voices carried from within. No sound at all, actually, which seemed wrong for a meeting between old friends.

"Mercy?" He pushed the door open wider, stepping into the empty office.

She wasn't there.

Zane's gaze swept the small space, cataloging details. An overturned chair. Papers scattered across the floor. Scuff marks on the carpet that could have been from a struggle.

His heated blood turned to ice.

He crossed the small office in three quick strides to the window, pressing his palms against the reinforced glass. The view overlooked the main landing platform, and what he saw there made his vision go red around the edges.

Mercy was being dragged across the tarmac by two pirates he recognized from their captivity. Her hands were bound in front of her, and she fought their grip with the fierce determination he'd come to know so well. But she was outnumbered, overpowered by men twice her size.

Captain Horris walked beside them, his scarred face split by a satisfied grin. And there, bringing up the rear like this was perfectly normal business, was Myles Judd.

The betrayal raked over Zane like enemy fire. Mercy had trusted Judd. Had called him friend. Had walked into his office believing she was safe.

Instead, she'd been sold out.

Rage exploded through Zane's chest, dragon fire racing along his nerves. The window glass cracked under his grip, hairline fractures spreading outward from his fingers. Heat poured off his skin in waves, and he could taste smoke on the back of his tongue.

They had his mate. They were taking her to that ship where they'd drain every drop of blood from her body for some treasure map encoded in her DNA.

Not happening.

Zane turned and ran. Through the office, down the corridor, out the nearest exit that led to the landing platform. His feet barely touched the ground as he sprinted across the tarmac, closing the distance between him and the group of pirates.

One of the pirates noticed him coming and shouted a warning. Horris spun around, his expression shifting from satisfaction to alarm as he took in Zane's approach. The man was smart enough to recognize a dragon in full protective fury.

Smart enough to be afraid.

Twenty yards between them. Close enough.

Zane launched himself into the air, his body already shifting before he reached the apex of his jump. Bones stretched and reformed. Scales erupted across his skin in waves of gold and red. Wings unfurled as he completed the transformation, casting a shadow across the entire landing platform.

His roar shook the air itself, a sound of pure

rage that sent smaller creatures scurrying for cover. Below him, the pirates scattered like insects, abandoning their captive as they dove for whatever cover they could find.

Except for Horris, who was apparently too stupid to run.

The pirate captain produced a massive blaster and began firing plasma bolts at Zane's exposed belly. The shots sizzled past, close enough that Zane could feel their heat. One connected with his left wing, sending pain lancing through the membrane. He rolled right, diving toward the platform with claws extended.

More weapons fire erupted from the pirate ship itself. Someone inside had activated the vessel's defensive systems, and energy beams sliced through the air where Zane had been moments before.

Those could do real damage if they connected. Could potentially kill him if they hit something vital.

He pulled up sharply, wings straining against the sudden change in direction. The ship's gunner tracked his movement, spraying fire across his flight path. Zane rolled left, then right, staying ahead of the targeting system through pure speed and agility.

But he couldn't keep this up forever. And every second he spent dodging gave them more time to secure Mercy.

Below, he caught sight of her breaking free from the chaos. She'd somehow gotten loose from her restraints and was running toward a cluster of maintenance equipment.

Good. His mate was getting herself to safety while he dealt with the immediate threats.

Then one of the pirates on the platform swung his weapon toward her fleeing form.

The sight of a blaster aimed at Mercy triggered something primal in Zane's hindbrain. Something that cared nothing for strategy or consequences or his own safety. His mate was threatened. Everything else became secondary.

He folded his wings and dove.

Dragon fire erupted from his throat in a torrent of superheated plasma. The first blast caught the pirate targeting Mercy, reducing him to ash before he could pull the trigger. The second engulfed two more pirates who'd been foolish enough to remain on the platform. The third turned a section of tarmac to molten slag.

The ship's defensive systems swiveled toward his

new position. Zane tried to pull up, tried to regain altitude before they could lock onto him. He almost made it.

The laser caught him along his left side, searing through scales and into the muscle beneath. Agony exploded along his flank, white-hot pain that disrupted his flight rhythm. His wing folded involuntarily, and suddenly, he was falling rather than flying.

The impact with the platform drove the breath from his lungs and sent fresh waves of pain through his injured side. He tried to maintain dragon form, tried to keep the advantage of size and natural weapons. But the damage was too severe. His body reverted to human shape without his conscious control, leaving him bleeding on the scorched tarmac.

His left arm hung uselessly at his side, the flesh blackened and blistered from the energy weapon. Every breath sent fire through his ribs. He could taste blood on his tongue.

But he was alive. And most of the pirates were very much not.

Horris and Myles Judd emerged from behind a piece of maintenance equipment, both pointing blasters at Zane's chest. They were close. Even injured, he might survive the shots, but he wasn't sure how much more damage he could absorb.

"You should have minded your own business, dragon," Horris snarled. His scarred face was flushed with anger and what might have been fear. "Now you get to watch your lady friend bleed out nice and slow."

"The bounty didn't say anything about you," Myles added, though his hands shook as he kept his weapon trained on Zane.

Zane tried to push himself upright, ignoring the way his vision grayed around the edges. If he could get to his feet, if he could summon enough fire to take them both out before they pulled their triggers …

"Zane, down!"

Mercy's voice cut through the haze of pain and rage. He threw himself flat against the platform without hesitation, trusting her completely even though he couldn't see what she had planned.

Twin blaster shots sizzled through the air where his head had been moments before.

Horris stumbled backward, a smoking hole in his chest where his heart used to be. Myles Judd crumpled to his knees, his weapon clattering across the tarmac as he clutched at the massive burn that had replaced most of his torso.

Mercy stood twenty feet away, a fallen pirate's las rifle still smoking in her hands. Her clothes were torn and dirty, her face streaked with sweat and debris. But her eyes blazed with fierce satisfaction as she watched their enemies fall.

Beautiful. His mate was absolutely beautiful.

She dropped the rifle and ran to him, falling to her knees beside his injured form. Her hands hovered over his burns, afraid to touch but needing to assess the damage.

"How bad?" she asked, her voice steady despite the tears tracking down her cheeks.

"I'll live." The words came out rougher than he'd intended, his throat raw from dragon fire and impact trauma. "Are you hurt?"

"I'm fine. You came for me." She said it like she couldn't quite believe it. Like the idea of someone riding to her rescue was foreign and wonderful and terrifying all at once.

"Always." He reached up with his good hand to cup her face.

Then she was kissing him, fierce and desperate and full of everything she couldn't put into words.

Relief and gratitude and something even bigger, though neither of them was ready to name it yet.

He kissed her back with all the passion his injured body could muster, pouring his own relief and devotion into her hold.

16

VEMION WAS nothing like Mercy had expected.

She pressed her face to the shuttle's viewport as they descended through atmosphere, watching alien landscapes unfold below. Not the gleaming cities or grand palaces she'd imagined, but vast wilderness stretching to every horizon. Mountains cloaked in forests so dense they looked like green velvet from altitude.

"It's beautiful," she murmured.

Zane's hand found hers, fingers intertwining with easy familiarity. His burns were healing with dragon swiftness, though angry red marks still traced his left side. "Wait until you see the rest."

The shuttle banked toward what looked like uninhabited wilderness. Trees gave way to a small clearing where a cabin sat nestled against the mountain's base. Not a palace or grand estate, but something that could have been lifted from her childhood dreams of home. Warm stone walls, wide windows that reflected the forest, all that was missing was smoke curling from a chimney into the crisp air.

"This is yours?" It wasn't exactly the home of a playboy lord.

"My retreat." The shuttle settled onto a landing pad that seemed carved from the mountainside itself. "When court gets too suffocating, I come here."

Mercy studied his profile as she powered down the systems. Away from the resort's luxury and the pirates' threats, he looked different. Relaxed in a way she'd never seen before. Like the masks he wore in civilized company had finally fallen away completely.

The air outside hit her lungs sharp and clean. It tasted of pine needles and mountain snow, wild in a way that made her chest expand with unexpected hunger. When had she last breathed air that hadn't been filtered through a dozen processors?

"Come on." Zane shouldered their single bag,

everything they'd managed to salvage from Saffron Court. "I'll show you around."

The cabin's interior matched its exterior. Comfortable furniture arranged around a stone fireplace. A kitchen that looked actually used rather than for show. Books scattered on tables like someone had been reading them recently. Everything spoke of a man who came here to be himself rather than impress anyone.

"You really live here?" She touched the spine of a worn technical manual, surprised to find it was about starship engines rather than seduction. Though Zane seemed to be a natural at *that*.

"When I can." He moved around the space with familiarity, lighting the fire with a gesture that sent dragon flame dancing across the logs. "Most of my family thinks I'm slumming it when I come out here. I do have a place closer to civilization, but that's …" He just shook his head instead of finishing the thought.

Mercy walked to the wide windows that looked out over the valley. The view stole her breath again. Nothing but forest and mountains and sky, with no sign of people anywhere. No traffic, no cities, no reminders of the outside universe.

"It's perfect."

"Is it?" Something in his voice made her turn. He stood by the fireplace, firelight playing across his features, and his expression held uncertainty she'd never seen before. "I know it's not what you're used to. Not much to do here except exist."

The doubt in his voice broke something open in her chest. This powerful dragon lord, this man who commanded fire and flew across battlefields to save her, was worried she might not like his sanctuary.

"Zane." She crossed to him, drawn by an instinct she was still learning to trust. "I've spent my entire adult life in metal boxes floating through a vacuum. This is ..." She gestured toward the windows, the fireplace, the simple comfort of it all. "This is the most beautiful place I've ever seen."

Relief flickered across his features. Had he really thought she'd find his retreat lacking? Did he not understand that she'd lived her whole life in spaces barely large enough for one person?

"I need to apologize." His words came out formally, weighted with something heavier than simple regret. "For lying to you. About what I was, about why I was on your ship. You deserved honesty from the beginning."

Mercy settled into the chair across from his, close enough to touch but giving them both space to think. "You weren't exactly in a position to trust me with your secrets on first meeting."

"It went beyond that." He stared into the fire, dragon flames reflecting in his eyes. "I've spent so long playing roles, being what people expected, that I forgot how to just be honest. Even when it mattered. Even with you."

The confession hit deep. She thought of all the times she'd sensed he was holding back, hiding parts of himself behind charm and careful words. Had wondered what secrets he carried and why he seemed reluctant to let her see past his surface.

"I owe you an apology too." The admission felt like swallowing glass. "For not trusting you when it counted."

Zane's gaze snapped to her face. "You had every reason to doubt. My reputation isn't exactly pristine."

"Your reputation isn't you." She reached for his hand, needing the contact to ground herself. "I should have known better. Should have trusted what I felt instead of what someone else told me to feel."

His fingers tightened around hers, warm and solid and real. "What did you feel?"

The question hung between them, simple words that demanded honesty she'd spent decades avoiding. But sitting here in his sanctuary, surrounded by the evidence of who he really was beneath all the masks, she found the truth easier than expected.

"Safe." The word came out quietly. "For the first time in twenty years, I felt safe. Not just protected, but … accepted. Yours."

Zane shifted forward, bringing them close enough that she could feel the heat radiating from his skin. His free hand cupped her face, thumb brushing across her cheekbone with devastating gentleness.

"You are." Each word carried absolute conviction. "You're my mate."

The term made her stomach flutter with something between excitement and terror. "What does that mean exactly?" She was here. She'd chosen him.

But perhaps there were a few things she should have clarified *before* jumping on the rented shuttle and coming to his secret hideaway.

"It means permanent." His eyes flickered with dragon fire, but his touch remained gentle. "You're not getting rid of me."

She was close to shaking. "I've never had a family." The confession slipped out before she could stop it. "Never had anyone who chose to stay. I don't know how to do this."

"Neither do I." His smile was soft, self-deprecating. "I've spent thirty years avoiding commitment. The irony isn't lost on me that the universe decided to make the choice for us."

"So what happens now?"

Instead of answering with words, he kissed her. Soft and sweet and full of promise.

When they broke apart, his eyes held flames that danced with something warmer than desire. "I think we start there."

He held out his hand, and she took it and let him lead her to the bedroom.

NEED A LITTLE MORE OF ZANE & MERCY?

Sign up at the link below to **receive a free bonus epilogue!**

Get your free bonus epilogue!

https://katerudolph.net/index.php/zane-bonus/

———

Thank you so much for reading *Zane*!

Your support means the world to me. If you enjoyed the story, it would mean even more if you could take a moment to share your thoughts in a review or leave a rating.

Hearing from readers like you makes all the difference!

———

Get more shifter goodness in Hunting Season! Flip the page for a preview.

This werewolf will protect his mate.

Owen has one job: keep Stasia from being abducted. Easier said than done when his fiercely independent client tries to fire him the moment they meet. His werewolf senses howl to life and he's certain of one thing: Stasia is his.

She's sick of cocky men.

When her wealthy father hires a bodyguard, Stasia says no. Not exactly a smart move after someone tried to nab her off the street. But she doesn't need a babysitter. Especially not a cheerfully overbearing bodyguard who makes her heart pound and her fantasies run wild.

When Stasia is yanked out of her glittering world and into Owen's she'll need to grapple with an impossible new reality that includes werewolves, silver bullets, and fated mates. Is she ready to embrace her new world?

Or will she run back to a universe of glittering high rises and leave her destiny behind? Step into the world of Guarded by the Shifter where a team of ex-military bodyguards are also werewolves and fated mates are just one job away.

INTERGALACTIC DATING
AGENCY

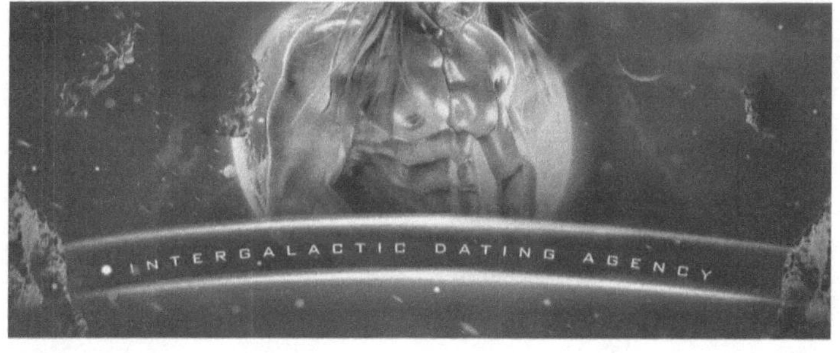

LOOKING for love that's out of this world? These strong, smart, sexy aliens are seeking mates from the Milky Way. Just hop onboard with your local Intergalactic Dating Agency. Join our group of authors as we explore the friendly skies and beyond with trilogies of cosmic craving, astral adventure, and otherworldly lovers. Warning: abductions may or may not be included!

Dragon Brides
Dragon Princes. Fierce Women. Love.
Fated mates, fierce women, and dragon princes are ready to find their mates.

Crux

Ranger

Saber

Cipher

Storm

Drake

Asher

Knox

Flint

Pine

Rook
Vex
Zane

Drakarn Mates

A harsh desert planet. Stranded humans. Draconic aliens. A match made in… well, somewhere.

Claimed by the Drakarn Warrior Lord
Echoes of Fire
Scorched by Fate
Fated to the Drakarn Commander
Chained to the Champion
Beast of Blood and Ash

Guarded by the Shifter

Werewolf. Bodyguard. Mate.

The origins of these shifters are shrouded in mystery, but they're determined to protect their mates from any harm that comes their way.

Also available in audio!
Hunting Season
On the Prowl
Stalking Magic
Hungry for the Wolf
Wolf Cursed (novella)
Wolf's Temptation

———

Stealing the Alpha

The thief takes what she wants, but the alpha keeps what's his...

Join shifter thief Mel as she clashes with lion alpha Luke in an explosive trilogy of two opposites who can't keep away from one another.

Also available in audio!
The Alpha Heist
Entangled with the Thief
In the Alpha's Bed

———

Alien Mates: Planet Exile

Guerran is no place for pretty human women. But these alien heroes will protect their mates!
Also available in audio!

Exile's Hunter
Exile's Adored

———

Zulir Warrior Mates

Kidnapped humans. Alien Warriors. Electric wings.
The Zulir Warrior Mates series brings you human heroines and heroes abducted from Earth who find love – and wings! – with the alien warriors who rescue them.
Also available in audio!

Synnr's Saint
Synnr's Hope
Synnr's Spark
Synnr's Kiss
Synnr's Ride

———

Mated to the Alien

Fated Mate Alien Romance

Detyens are doomed to die young if they don't find their fated mates.

Follow along as these mated pairs fight off aliens, corrupt dictators, prejudiced humans, pirates, and more! The books can be read or listened to in any order, though some characters show up in multiple stories.

Select books available in audio.

Pick a book and jump into the action today!

Ruwen

Tyral

Stoan

Cyborg

Krayter

Kayleb

Shayn

Braxtyn

Doryan

Dekon

Detyen Warriors

Detya was destroyed a hundred years ago. These doomed warriors are out to find justice… and their mates.

The Detyen Warriors series brings you kick butt heroines, alpha alien heroes, fated mates, and relationships strong enough to span the galaxy!

The entire series is also available in audio!

Soulless

Ruthless

Heartless

Faultless

Endless

Detyen Warrior Outcasts
Fated Mate Alien Romance

These doomed warriors were abandoned by their people and live on the edge. Their mates hold the key to their salvation.

Pick a book and jump into the action today!

Dangerous Bond

Intrepid Bond

Wayward Bond

Alien Holiday Romance

Christmas… in space????
These alien holiday romances look beyond Earth's winter holidays and ring in the season across the galaxy!
Select titles available in audio.
Snowed in with the Alien Beast
The Alien's Winter Gift
The Alien Reindeer's Wild Ride
Trapped with her Alien Mate

Alien Outlaws

Outlaws, schemes, and love… it's all there in the Alien Outlaws series…
Andie Munster is sick of life on Ixilta, the planet she got dumped on after being abducted from Earth six years ago. And when the mysterious and dangerous Xandr shows up looking for a way off the planet, she's half-prisoner, half-co-conspirator in a wild rush to escape.

Rogue Alien's Escape
Rogue Alien's Woman
Rogue Alien's Secret
Rogue Alien's Legacy

———

Find more by Kate Rudolph at www.katerudolph.net

ABOUT KATE RUDOLPH

KATE RUDOLPH IS a paranormal and sci-fi romance writer who lives in Indiana. She loves writing about kick butt heroines and the steamy heroes who love them. She's been devouring romance novels since she was too young to be reading them and had to hide her books so no one would take them away. She couldn't imagine a better job in this world than writing romances and sharing them with her fellow readers.

If you enjoyed this story, please consider leaving a review.

www.ingramcontent.com/pod-product-compliance
Lightning Source LLC
Chambersburg PA
CBHW021148190726

48288CB00008B/2872